THE COAST

John Enright

Books by John Enright

FICTION
The Coast
Some People Talk with God
New Jerusalem News
Blood Jungle Ballet
The Dead Don't Dance
Fire Knife Dancing
Pago Pago Tango

POETRY
14 Degrees South

THE COAST

John Enright

Black Heron Press
Post Office Box 614
Anacortes, Washington 98221
www.blackheronpress.com

Copyright © 2024 by John Enright. All rights reserved.
All of the characters in this book are fictitious. Any resemblance to persons living or dead is entirely coincidental. No part of this book may be reproduced in any manner without written permission from the publisher except in the case of brief quotations embedded in critical articles and reviews.

ISBN (print): 978-1-936364-42-8
ISBN (ebook): 978-1-936364-43-5

Cover art and design by Bryan Sears.

1966

Chapter 1

Morey was pissed. Well, screw Morey. Patrick was just following the signs. How was he to know—middle of the night, Morey sound asleep in the back—that he shouldn't have taken the turn-off that said San Francisco/Golden Gate Bridge but kept on straight for Oakland and some other bridge? Patrick had never been here before. So, it was longer? They'd been on the road for almost three days, what was another half hour or so? Plus, there was less traffic, almost none this early in the morning, just a state road not a freeway.

Diane went back to sleep mode, curled up on the front seat beside him, under her afghan, her head in his lap. She was afraid of Morey, thought he was creepy, and she had stuck by Patrick the whole trip. Morey and Patrick had taken turns driving. Well, Patrick had done most of the driving. After all, that was why Morey had taken him on, that and splitting the gas money. Diane was just splitting the gas money. She didn't drive. They had both found Morey through the ride board at Columbia. Diane went to school there, Barnard. Patrick didn't.

It was a ten-year-old, oil-burning '56 Ford station wagon, black and white, with lousy alignment so that it started shimmying at 60. Morey had a New York street-vendors hot-dog steam table strapped to the roof rack. There was no back seat, just a mattress and piles of stuff. When Patrick drove, Diane sat in front with him. When Morey took over, she went in the back with Patrick. After sharing the mattress a couple of times, they started making out. It seemed like the natural thing to do. The car started weaving a bit, back and forth. It was Diane spotted Morey, watching them in the twisted-down rearview mirror and jerking off.

When they got to the north end of the bridge, swooping down to it through tunnels and curves, the sun was just rising, washing the pastel city across from them in soft pink and shadows. For the past thirty-six hours Patrick had been running on speed, the little white pills Morey would pass to Diane to give him along with a small Dixie cup of Scotch. San Francisco looked like fucking heaven, a fresh, flesh-colored Jerusalem. Diane was awake now, smiling. "Home," she said.

First stop was to drop Diane off, a neighborhood not far from the end of the bridge, a street of substantial, nearly identical, pastel row houses. She gave Patrick a kiss and her phone number when he helped her get her bag from the back. She paid Morey for her third of the gas, as did Patrick for his. Morey drove from there. He asked Patrick, Where to? Patrick had an address, friends of a friend, but Morey said that was too far out of his way and dropped Patrick and his backpack off on Market Street, the main drag. Patrick walked, a free man. He found a diner and had a big breakfast. Excellent coffee.

That was Patrick's Bay Area baptism, the start of the affair. He was twenty. He had gotten himself on unemployment by shaving his head at his last job. That was enough to get him fired. When he discovered he could collect his forty-eight dollars a week in any state, he traded Manhattan for San Francisco. It was the summer before the summer that came to be called the Summer of Love. San Francisco was still a blue-collar, union town. Oh, there were wealthy pockets, just as there were poor ethnic neighborhoods, but the city itself was still mainly working class. Much of the military cargo for the growing war in Southeast Asia departed from its docks. A taste of its origins as a frontier, gold-rush town still lingered. The ghost of Bogart's Sam Spade still stalked its foggy after-midnight streets.

It was a city for walkers, and Patrick took to that. The friends of a friend were not friendly. They let him stay just a couple of nights. He found a place to crash with people he met through a friend of Diane's, a sort of group house near Golden Gate Park. He wasn't sure why he was here. He could give no explanation. There was no name to what he was looking for. There was nothing behind that he was fleeing. When Diane asked, he said he was just exploring. He walked the city.

They called it a commune, but it didn't have a name. It was just *the house.* Patrick's contribution to the house was their daily bread. There was a bakery over in the Mission District that sold its day-old bread for ten cents a loaf. Every couple of days he would hike over there and bring back as much as he could carry in his backpack. It wasn't much of a hike, just a mile or so each way. The bread was his contribution to the commune. In return, they let him sleep and eat there. Sometimes, if the bakery had them, he would buy expired doughnuts too.

LSD was not yet illegal. There was a tall dude who dressed like Dracula in a cape and walked a pair of wolf hounds around the neighborhood, and who supposedly was the source of most of it. Acid was hard to avoid. It was like a cult. The other people in the house were often tripping and made no secret of it. They were all older than Patrick. He thought of them as middle-aged. They had all left something behind to be there—jobs, kids, marriages, careers. They were all weird, as far as Patrick was concerned, harmless and nice enough, but weird. They all smiled too much for one thing, smiles like masks. Sometimes he couldn't make sense of what they were saying. He'd smile back and nod. That always seemed to work, as if it really didn't matter. The communication was all inside their heads.

You had to be careful what you drank, you couldn't just drink something out of the fridge. They would spike anything. Members of the cult did not proselytize with words, they converted with doses. Patrick wasn't interested, and it made no difference to his housemates if he was tripping or not—they were. They especially liked to acid-lace the sangria they fixed, cheap dago-red wine with spices and fruit, and go off together. To Patrick it was like a sci-fi zombie movie or something. He drank only beer, and they thought him weird.

Patrick did like pot, however, and what Diane came up with was better than the New York ganja he was used to. Diane and Patrick were not an item. She had a boyfriend for one thing, Helmut, who had connected him to the house and was also the source of her dope. When they got stoned together, Helmut could do a very accurate and funny impersonation of an older, lost-in-the-cosmos acidhead. Helmut also had a car, and they'd all three go for drives. Helmut confessed to Patrick that he liked having him along because, truth to tell, he often found Diane boring.

Patrick was a New York kid. He wasn't use to having the country so close. Just back across the Golden Gate were the huge trees and twisting roads of Marin, the empty hills and forest-tunneled canyons. And an ocean that was not Jones Beach. Helmut took them there, to a saloon in a little coastal village called Bolinas. It was where Helmut scored his marijuana. It was like some other country, like country squared or risen to another power. These folks wanted to retreat into time, not go on. They had stepped backwards off the edge. They weren't smiling like the acidheads, even though the saloon was called Smiley's. They seemed a tad snappish and stand-offish, a brand of wild-west demeanor, even their clothing. Maybe it was because the three of them were strangers and obviously city folk, the them to their us. This was not exactly a tourist town or a tourist's saloon. Serious pool was being played for drinks. Patrick wasn't old enough to drink in California, but no one cared. Diane didn't like the place and went for a walk.

A week or so later, by himself, Patrick hitchhiked back to Bolinas. It didn't take long. Californians were generous with rides, and hitchhikers were so common that cops pretty much ignored you. He only had to walk the last mile or so from the coast road into the village, around a wild-shored, placid lagoon. There was no road sign at the cut-off to Bolinas, as the villagers would disappear any sign the highway department put up. There were a lot of birds, no traffic.

Once again, he had no real reason for going there, just exploring. One explored best alone. He had just cashed his unemployment check. He could say he was looking for work. You always had to sign that you were looking for work before they handed over your check. He was wearing his backpack. He could hardly have left his stuff at the house. It would have become communal property. The fog was coming in. Patrick hadn't figured out the fog yet. It just seemed to roll in whenever it pleased, and it was pleasing. It felt clean, and it made the world more private.

He went to Smiley's. He didn't draw much attention this time, maybe because he was alone, maybe because he had obviously hiked in. He propped his pack in a corner. Midafternoon on a foggy day, there weren't many other patrons, just a handful of men and a woman at the bar and an old man who looked like Walt Whitman at a corner table playing chess against himself. Patrick ordered a tall can of Rainier Ale, what the locals called green death. No one spoke to him. They weren't talking to each other either. They were meditative quiet, Zen drinkers. The bartender and the woman were both reading books.

About halfway through his ale, a slight jingling sound came up, like little chimes. The backbar bottles were jiggling together. The bartender looked up and put down his paperback. The woman kept reading but picked up her drink. Down the bar, the men held onto their cans of green death. Within a second the shaking started. Walt Whitman's chess pieces danced to new squares and the loaded flypaper strips hanging from the ceiling swayed together. A bowling alley sound came from above them. A door somewhere slammed shut. Then, just like that, it stopped, with a few departing creaks and building moans.

No one said anything. No one had moved. The bartender surveyed his bottles. Walt studied his rearranged chess board. The woman took a sip and turned a page. "Fucking fault," she said. Patrick finished his ale and ordered another. She was not young—graying temples—but she was youthful, tanned and sinewy, sharp featured. There were many rings on her long fingers.

It wasn't but a few minutes before a young girl in pigtails came running in. "Mom, did you feel it?"

"Of course I felt it. You didn't have to run all the way down here to ask me that."

"But, mom, the pipe came down again. The water's everywhere."

"Ah Jesus fucking Christ," she said. "He said it was in there for good. God damn it." She shut her book and finished her drink. She looked down the bar at the men sitting there, then shook her head. She picked up her change from the bar and got up to go. Then she saw Patrick at the end of the bar. "You're not doing anything. Come on. Those drunks are useless."

"It's the San Andreas," Joanna told him. "This is where it comes back on land after leaving San Francisco, right up the lagoon. It shakes here often, especially recently." They were seated on the front stoop of her house, sipping mugs of Everclear and cranberry juice. They were both dripping wet, soaked to the bone, but the pipe was back where it belonged. The pipe connected the cistern that collected rainwater from her tin roof to the plumbing in the house, a gravity feed.

There wasn't much water left in the cistern now. "Hope it rains tonight," she said.

There was a separate one-room cabin behind Joanna's house. Patrick ended up staying there, at first for the night until his clothes dried out, but the next day was foggy and damp and they never did. He had dry things in his pack to wear, of course, but Joanna wouldn't let him pack wet clothes. The daughter's name was Daisy, or maybe it wasn't. She wasn't sure. "I'm still metamorphous. You know, between forms, like a caterpillar. I think I'll only be Daisy for a while." She said that she was ten in adult years. "But they're not the same, you know." She wasn't around much.

As far as Patrick could tell, there were just the two of them. The second day was sunny, and he hung his damp stuff up again to dry. Then he hiked back down to town with Joanna. She called the area where she lived the mesa, a plateau above the waterside main street with scattered, simple, one-story places like hers. They didn't take one lane because, Joanna said, "There's a nasty guard goose down there. Not worth the hassle." Joanna was as tall as Patrick, so she seemed taller, and she wore a battered Panama hat that added to that. She was another escaped New Yorker, grew up there and had lived only there before coming west. She asked Patrick about the city. It had been fifteen years.

They stopped at the post office so she could check her P.O. box, then to a sort of country bodega. Joanna put only a few essentials into her basket. "Expecting a check that wasn't there," she said with a shrug.

"What else you need? I've got some cash," Patrick said.

Joanna gave him a look, then nodded. She added a half

dozen more items, including a packet of Twinkies. "For Daisy," she said.

A week later Patrick was still there. He hitchhiked back to San Francisco to pick up his next unemployment check, but he left his pack behind. He picked up a few things Joanna had asked for, including a book from a bookstore in North Beach. There were things to do around Joanna's place. For instance, the cabin roof leaked. Patrick wasn't much of a carpenter, but he tried to fix it. Shingles were missing. There was an abandoned gardening shack at the back of her property with an intact roof. With Joanna's permission, he borrowed part of it. She had a hammer, but he had to buy the nails. An overloaded bookshelf in her house was listing dangerously. He repaired it, and he replaced two rotted-out steps up to her back door.

He also wandered around the mesa and Bolinas, and hitchhiked farther north along the coast, up to Pt. Reyes and Bodega Bay. Wherever he could he went to the shore, the cliffs or the coves. There was an endless empty wild beach at Pt. Reyes. He bought food for the house, and Joanna cooked. When she was there. She was gone a lot. Daisy came and went. No agreement was reached; no plans were made. It was just day-to-day. Some nights he'd get stoned and listen to the music Joanna was playing up in the house. She played a lot of different things, always ending with the same piano concerto.

One afternoon Joanna asked Patrick if he wanted to go to the city. She was getting a ride in to attend some event.

He put on what he thought of as his city clothes and went with her. There were two other people, the driver, a thin guy who didn't talk, just drove, and a man named Barry, whom Patrick had seen around the village and seemed scared of Joanna, or at least super-deferential. There was a choice of two roads south to the Golden Gate, one along the coastal cliffs, the other inland through the hills, both two-lane and a toss-up as to which had more curves. As with most public binary choices, each side had its adamant advocates. Fatality rates and accident anecdotes bolstered both sides. Genderwise, it seemed to Patrick, women preferred the inland route and men the coast. Their driver headed for the hills, maybe because there was a woman aboard.

The place was called The Spaghetti Factory. It was in North Beach. There was a bar and a big, high-beamed dining room, more like a hall, the old factory floor. Joanna hadn't mentioned what sort of event it was. There was nothing going on when they got there, but the place was pretty full and no one was eating, just drinking. There was no one way to describe the crowd. Eclectic? Well, there were no suits. An older crowd, casual but not relaxed. There were as many women as men. There was a smattering of caveman types, but also those groomed for regular jobs. There was loud talk and laughter and the blue haze of exhaled smoke. Joanna and Barry disappeared into the crowd.

Patrick went to the bar and ordered an Anchor Steam. No one had said anything about a ride back. He didn't feel comfortable—too many people, all of whom knew why they were there while he didn't know what he was doing with them. But if he followed his instinct to leave and prowl North Beach, he might not be able to hook up with Joanna and the ride back. For all he knew, Joanna wouldn't be going back tonight. He didn't feature hitching back in the dark. There would be no traffic anyway. Could he crash back at the old house or at Diane's? In any event, he had to get out of here.

He walked up to Coit Tower, but there were tourist busses there and more people. He hiked down the steps on the harbor side, as usual headed for the water. There was always a new side to this city of many sides. He walked the Embarcadero along the docks. The port was busy. It was late afternoon, and shifts were changing. For some reason, being among these people did not discomfort him. They were not just standing around like the tourist herds or the folks at the beer hall. They were moving, flowing like water in a stream. He was used to the streets of New York, where everything human was always in motion, in separate, personal, private motion.

It was dusk by the time Patrick got back to The Spaghetti Factory, and North Beach had turned on its lights, waking up for night life. Inside, some sort of meeting was going on. A man with a striking resemblance to George Armstrong Custer was making a speech, reading it. Patrick went to the bar, where there were empty stools now. He could see into the beer hall, a sea of backs and heads facing the far end. Patrick couldn't make out what the man was saying—he wasn't miked—and he didn't care. When this was over, he'd look for Joanna and see what was up.

Applause. Maybe this would be over soon. But no. No one was leaving. Another speaker was being introduced, a woman. It was Joanna, greeted by polite applause. She didn't speak long, only a couple of minutes. Again, Patrick could not hear clearly what she was saying. She ended by reading a poem. He could tell by her pauses. It wound down after that. Some announcements, one of which had to be a joke because it was greeted by laughter. There was a crush at the bar then, and Patrick finished his beer and left. He'd wait for Joanna out front.

He was a medium-sized guy in a tan doeskin jacket, a graying ponytail. Joanna was trying to ignore him. He was following her, talking at her back as they exited with the crowd. Joanna saw Patrick standing by the curb and came to him. "Seen Barry or Slim?" she asked. Patrick just shook his head. He was watching the man behind her, who was hard to ignore. A weathered face, a wispy ginger-colored moustache and goatee, drunken eyes. He was asking questions. Joanna didn't look frightened or angry, just resigned. The man put a hand on her shoulder, and she shrugged it off. The second time he did it, Patrick stepped forward.

"Just ignore him," Joanna said.

"Beat it," Patrick said.

"Oh, an even younger cub this time," the man said.

"Get lost, Peter," Joanna said, still not turning around. "Go find yourself."

Patrick took another step forward, so that he was standing beside Joanna, and the guy took a step backwards.

"Yeah, right, get lost. Not that simple, Jo. Not that simple at all. I meant what I said. I'll make you regret it." He left. Barry showed up; he was not going back with them. "Was that Peter?" he asked. A few minutes later Slim pulled up in the car. There was silence all the way back to Bolinas.

Chapter 2

"Are you registered for the draft, Patrick?" A strange question, out of nowhere. Patrick was at the top of the ladder, scooping tree gunk from the gutter filter. Joanna was at the base of the ladder, holding it. The gutter carried rainwater to the cistern. It was not a very sturdy ladder.

"Yeah."

"Where?"

"Back in Manhattan. Why?"

"Are you going to be drafted?"

"Up to them, not me. Don't know how I'd find out."

"By letter."

"To an address I left two years ago."

"Would you go if you did find out?"

"Don't know. Probably not."

"Why?"

"Not my war. Watch out." He tried to miss her with a load of gunk. It was a beautiful day. A turkey buzzard circled above them like a supervisor, traces of high fog like lacework dissolving in the sun.

"Did you stay around for any of the meeting?"

He shifted his weight, reaching out to finish the job, and the ladder slipped sideways.

"Come down. That's enough."

He did. "Nah. Couldn't hear much from the back. Went

for a walk."

"You might have been interested. It was about that war and what's being asked of your generation."

"I did catch your bit at the end, but I couldn't hear much of it. You read a poem."

"That's right. They asked me to."

They got the ladder down together.

"What was it called?"

"You can't tell a poem by its title."

"Okay. What was it about?"

"It's about the habits of denial and how to cook liver and onions," she said.

"That's about the war?"

"In a way. A poem can do that."

The war in Vietnam was becoming one of those things, a big thing that you were supposed to pay attention to and have an opinion about. The big things came and went, like the last one, the so-called Cuban missile crisis. Patrick ignored it. There was nothing he could do about it. It was just another adult fuck-up. The country sure seemed fond of being at war. He could not imagine himself as a soldier.

"Your peers are dying over there, for no good reason."

"Are you supposed to have a reason to die?" Patrick asked. He had trouble with that word peers. It wasn't a group he had ever joined. Hell, he had never joined any group, much less one called peers. He did not know anyone who had died over there. He had never been good at making friends. Why had they gone there? If you got shot, you probably bled to death. What was that like, watching your future drain out of you? Sacrifices were bled to death. There was something Talmudic about it. In your fading thoughts did you search for a reason?

"Offhand, I can't think of any thing or person I would die for," he said.

"Peacenik," Joanna said.

Joanna asked Patrick to stay. She would be gone for four or five days at least, another protest event down in L.A. She had farmed Daisy out. She wanted someone around the place while she was gone. It was that communal property thing again. Stuff left alone was in danger of being appropriated by someone who needed it more, or just wanted it. Unguarded meant nonessential. He could move up to the house. It wasn't like there was anywhere else he had to be.

Patrick had never been much of a reader. It was an attention-span thing—too many words—and it had always been presented as a chore, a punishment, homework. Reading was a necessary skill, like arithmetic, not entertainment. There were books in Joanna's house, books and records and her turntable stereo, no TV. Two slim books with her name on the cover were on the kitchen table, as if left out for him, books of poems. His second night in the house he fixed a pot of tea, rolled a joint, and sat down to look at them. He liked the way the words were spread across and down the page, not clumped together in black boxes. It reminded him of animal or bird tracks, something to follow. The open spaces were like pauses to stop and look around, the way wild things forage. The words were all ones he knew and used. There was nothing he didn't understand, but it was language stripped bare. One thought was not protected from the next. Very private things were said. It was like being inside someone else's brain, someone with a sense of humor who was sometimes angry, sometimes sad. He could only read a few pages at a time. He felt like a voyeur.

He slept in Joanna's bed. The only other place to sleep was Daisy's room. In order to advertise the fact that the house was occupied even if Joanna was not there, Patrick undertook some yardwork clearing. There was a thorny bramble plant that wanted to be the only plant. He didn't hurry; there was no rush. But removing it did become a bit of an obsession. The yard looked so much better with it gone, giving everything else a chance. Patrick had never done yard work before, simple gratification.

On the third or fourth day, Daisy reappeared. She'd had it with the Greysons, she said. "Talk about dysfunctional." She didn't help with the yardwork, but she took over some kitchen duties and pretty much kept to herself or out of the house. Joanna's four or five days away passed. Late one afternoon, as Patrick was finishing up in the side yard, a man in a familiar jacket strolled past the house. When he got a ways up their dirt lane, he stopped and strolled back. It was the man who had been bugging Joanna in North Beach. When he turned into the path to the front door, Patrick went to meet him.

"Can I help you?" Patrick asked.

"Yeah, mind your own business."

"Nobody's home." Patrick was shirtless, with a bandana tied across his forehead and wearing a pair of heavy work gloves.

"Nobody asked you." The man continued up the path.

Patrick cut him off, standing in front of the front steps. "What do you want?"

"I want you, whoever you are, to get out of my fucking way."

"No. What's your business here?"

The man took a long look at Patrick. Again, the bloodshot, squinting eyes, the smell of alcohol. He took a step backwards and called, "Daisy, come on out and say hello."

"I told you nobody's home."

"Fuck you," he said. Then he called out again, "Daisy, it's me. Let's talk."

"Daisy's not here. Now, let's go." Patrick pushed the man backwards with a hand on his chest.

The man stumbled backwards. "Alright, alright. You don't have to get tough about it." He left, mumbling.

When Daisy got home the first thing she asked was, "Was my father here?"

"I don't know who your father is," Patrick said.

"He was, wasn't he? I heard he was in town, looking for me. The Greysons are terrified of him."

"There was a man here looking for you."

"What did you tell him?"

"That you weren't here, that there was nobody here."

"Good. If I hide out down in the cabin, can you keep him away from me?"

"Sure, I guess. I can try, but…why?"

"'Cause, just 'cause. I don't have to see him."

Patrick went down to Smiley's that night. Daisy's father was there. He was quite drunk. Playing pool, he had to lean on the table to stay erect. He was playing for drinks. He kept winning. He spoke to no one. No one spoke to him. If he saw Patrick at all, he didn't recognize him.

When Joanna returned, Patrick moved back to the cabin and Daisy moved up to the house. Patrick mentioned to Joanna that the sole time he had to defend the homestead was when Daisy's father stopped by. "Oh?" was all she said. A few days later she told him that there were some people coming up from L.A. for a protest, and she would need the cabin to put them up. Patrick had been getting a bit too cozy there. Daisy had taken to calling him Uncle Rick. Joanna had the address of a cohort—her word—in Berkeley who rented out rooms to university students. It was summer break; maybe she had a place where he could crash.

Patrick had taken the two books of her poems down to the cabin. He was reading them slowly, a poem a night, two if they were short. Packed and ready to leave, he stopped at the house to return them. "No, keep them," Joanna said. "You can return them later." She wrote down the Berkeley name and address, a Naomi on Milvia Street, then she added her phone number. "Stay in touch," she said. "Don't be a stranger."

"Say adios to Daisy for me."

"I will."

Patrick had trouble hitching to Berkeley. Trouble? Hell, it couldn't be much more than forty miles, but it took him most of the day. He didn't want to go back through San Francisco. He'd head around the top of the bay. He got to Tam Junction in good time, in the back of a pickup truck. From there, not knowing really where he was going, he screwed up several times. He ended up doing a lot of walking, had to backtrack twice, got hassled by a cop in Larkspur, and was stranded for more than an hour at the San Quentin exit right before the Richmond Bridge. The prison was a scary looking place, a graceless, brooding, sprawling castle. A reverse castle, really—castles were meant to shelter the good inside the walls from the evil-doers outside. These high walls enclosed another type of courtyard.

In Berkeley it was another long hike from the freeway up to Milvia Street. He had to ask directions. Berkeley was different. Whereas in San Francisco the hills were integrated into the city, in Berkeley the hills had their own neighborhood on a ridgeline away from the bay. Milvia was at the base of those hills. Being a friend of Joanna's got Patrick a deal. Naomi assumed he was another cohort, in town on some mission. Patrick did not tell her otherwise. She had a space for him for free, well, just five bucks a week to cover the power and water.

Once again, he was out back, in the garage this time, a humble one-car garage whose door had been replaced by a line of salvaged, mismatched French doors. A small wooden, windowed garden shed was attached to one side. The garage was jail-house furnished, only everything was close to the floor, Japanese-style. An old door up on milk crates served as a table, with one short-legged rattan chair, woven-grass mats on the floor, some pillows, a small refrigerator, and a hotplate on a wo0den box with a pot and pan and dishes below. In the shed was another door up off the floor on cement blocks—the bed—and a small electric heater. There was an overhead light and a lamp on the table. Patrick gave Naomi five dollars and asked about a bathroom. There was a spigot outside the shed, he could piss in the yard, and he could use the bathroom in the house when he had to. The back door was always open.

Naomi was surprised that Patrick wasn't traveling with a sleeping bag and pad on his backpack.

"City boy," Patrick said.

"I could tell. New York? You sound like Joanna. There's a family resemblance, too. Related?"

"Not to my knowledge."

"I'll bring you a sleeping bag. You'll need it. They get left here."

Aside from her voice, there was little feminine about Naomi. A man's haircut, a loose Hawaiian shirt, cargo shorts, the way she walked, and how she held her arms flexed in front of her. Patrick would not have been surprised if she pulled a bag of Red Man out of a cargo pocket and tucked a chew in her cheek. She returned with not just a plush sleeping bag but also a pad to put beneath it and a couple of bed pillows.

"How's it looking for next weekend?" she asked. "Any problems?"

"Fine, I guess. No problems that I know of." Patrick had not the slightest idea what she was asking about.

Naomi answered with a chuckle, well, a snort. "You can trust me. Let me know if there's anything I can do. Anyway, we'll be there."

Berkeley was boring, a university town slumbering in summer. The south campus side along Telegraph Avenue was interesting but occupied by weird people, so that you had to keep your defenses up. Panhandlers, buskers, more of those faraway acid smiles. A weirdo ghetto. He tried to buy beer, but got carded and had to leave. You could smell marijuana on the street, but he couldn't buy a beer. The lots, the houses, and he was sure the prices got bigger as you went uphill behind the campus. Faculty houses, boring. But the F bus would take him across the bridge to the city. He was drawn to it.

Patrick basically just slept at the garage. He saw little of Naomi whose bathroom he shared and whose washing machine he was allowed to use. One night when he got back late, on the last F bus, there was a note from Naomi duct-taped to the one French door that opened—*Call Joanna.*

His mornings had come to begin with a coffee and pastry at Pete's up on the avenue. He liked watching the young women who worked there, one in particular. He didn't know her name; he just watched her. He had learned to expect that any girl he found attractive was already in a relationship. It just figured. A woman was a prize, and most prizes were already taken. Prizes had to be stalked. He didn't know how.

He knew Joanna slept late, so he waited before calling. He called from the phone booth outside the Safeway. Joanna just wanted to know if he would be home at Naomi's today. They were headed into Oakland and she thought they might stop by. Daisy wanted to say hello. Patrick, as usual, had no plans. He asked what time. A couple of hours, she said. Guests! On the way back to Naomi's he stopped in some shops along the avenue and got cheese and bread, a peach and some apples, and a quart of fresh lemonade.

Patrick hadn't thought to tell Joanna that he was in the garage, so he was waiting on Naomi's front steps when Slim pulled up. Slim stayed in the car.

"Slim is an antisocial socialist," Joanna said as they walked back up the driveway.

"Slim is a shithead," Daisy said.

Patrick gestured to his humble abode, its wall of mismatched French doors. "My villa," he said.

"Ah, Villa Auto," Joanna said. Daisy took to the place immediately.

Joanna couldn't stay long. She had an event in Oakland to attend. But she had some cheese and bread and apple while Daisy explored.

"Just wanted to check on how you were getting along."

"Want your books back?"

"Books? What books? Oh, those. No, hang onto them."

Daisy was out in the side yard, checking things out, leaving them alone. She wasn't hungry, she said.

"A shame taking her away to this boring adult thing I'm going to. I couldn't leave her at home because her father's in town. Say, could I leave her here with you, pick her up later? She seems to think you're okay, for an adult. You could show her around Berkeley. She's never been here before."

This did not strike Patrick as a request expecting a negative answer. "Sure," he said.

So, Daisy was staying. They walked Joanna out to the car, where Slim hadn't moved from his driver's seat. No kisses or hugs, just an irritated "Wait, mom," from Daisy, who opened the back door, pulled out a kid's yellow school backpack and slammed the door shut. "Bye, mom," she said.

Back in the villa, Daisy tore into the bread and cheese and fruit like a child who hadn't eaten in days. "That's good lemonade," she said. "Thanks for agreeing, Uncle Rick. I had to get out of town. Nowhere to hide."

"No problem," Patrick said. He was eyeing her dirty yellow backpack, which looked stuffed.

"Mom didn't think you would go for it, but I thought you might."

"What exactly have I gone in for?"

"Why, letting me stay with you until dad is gone. Didn't she explain it to you?"

"Your mother just said she wanted to leave you here while she went to her event, then pick you up later."

"She didn't say when later, did she?"

"No."

"That's mom."

Chapter 3

Naomi wouldn't hear of it. That's after she heard of it. Patrick had gone up to the house to ask if she had another sleeping bag. When she asked what for, he had to tell her. There was no way she would let him keep a young girl in her garage. Joanna's daughter? She would sleep up here in the house. Daisy went for it. "I wasn't featuring sleeping on that door."

The next morning, Daisy emerged bathed and changed, and her hair was no longer in pigtails but pulled back in a ponytail. The tails of a woman's life—fairy tales to pigtails to ponytails to cocktails and hightails to folk tales. Daisy might be sleeping and grooming at Naomi's, but she was hanging out with Uncle Rick. She had brought books to read and seemed content to just do that. But Patrick had to move, get out of the garage, and she came with him.

Berkeley was less boring with Daisy along. She was interested in everything and asked a lot of questions, many of which Patrick couldn't answer. Telegraph was a circus for her. She was constantly hungry. He bought her a T-shirt she wanted with a big green marijuana leaf stenciled on it. She wanted pizza for dinner.

It was dusk when they got back to the villa. They had stopped at the Safeway for supplies. Patrick could not afford many more days of feeding Daisy out. Naomi came down when she saw their lights were on. She brought news. Joanna had been arrested. A sit-in at the Oakland Selective Service office. Naomi had been there. They had arrested everyone up in front and taken them inside. No word on where they had taken her or when she could get out.

Daisy did not take this well. "Poor mom! Can you imagine being locked inside a cell? Did they hurt her? Hit her or anything?"

"I didn't see that she was hit, but they had to drag her away because she refused to stand up."

"The pigs."

"I'll let you know if I hear anything. You come up to bed. Have you eaten?"

The next day was Sunday, which generally didn't mean anything, but Naomi reported that because it was Sunday, Joanna and the others would not be arraigned until Monday at the earliest. She was in the Alameda County Jail. Patrick took Daisy to San Francisco to get her mind off it. It was the idea of her mom being locked in a room that bothered her most.

"You ever been locked up, Uncle Rick?"

"Never, thank god."

"That's gotta be the worst."

They were on the F bus crossing the Oakland Bay Bridge. The white puffs of clouds in the sky were matched by the blotches of darker blue on the bay. On the second span, after Treasure Island, the San Francisco waterfront opened up. You could see it better from the bus, above the guardrails and traffic. On the off-ramp from the bridge, the always-morning aroma of fresh coffee from the Folger's factory seeped through the window cracks. They walked to North Beach through the Sunday-deserted Financial District, shared a bowl of noodles in Chinatcwn. They didn't talk much. There wasn't much to say.

Monday came and went with no word. Daisy read, sitting on pillows beneath the big redwood in the yard. Today she wasn't eating at all, as if on a hunger strike. Tuesday, word Joanna had been released, but nothing from her. Naomi reported that Joanna's name had been mentioned on the TV news. Hot-plate black beans and rice for dinner. Daisy broke her fast. Another three days like that. Daisy spent more time up in the house, where Naomi let her watch TV. Daisy had had little exposure to television—Joanna never owned one—so she had no immunity. Over dinner she'd retell an entire episode of *Bonanza*.

"Naomi's nice, but she's kind of dyke-y, you know? She's a vegetarian. Mom has a poem about people in denial about having incisors." She pointed to one of hers.

"Is that the poem about liver and onions?"

"No, another one."

It was Saturday before they heard from Joanna, or rather, Patrick heard from her. She left a message with Naomi for him to call her; she was home. He did, from the Safeway phone booth. He didn't tell Daisy her mother had called. He wasn't sure why, just a feeling. Naomi hadn't told her either.

"So, how's everything in Berkeley?" Joanna sounded casual.

"Okay. How's it with you?"

"Daisy okay?"

"She's alright, worried about you."

"I've been busy. Listen, it's clear for her to come home."

"That's good news."

"Can you bring her?"

"Don't know how. No busses to Bolinas, and I'm not hitchhiking with her."

"I'll see if I can get Slim to go pick her up. You come, too. The cabin's available."

"Her father's gone?"

"That's why I wanted to talk to you first. I'm having him arrested. I had a restraining order taken out on him last year, last time he showed up and caused trouble. I finally reported him. He was getting threatening. They're looking for him now. Listen, Patrick, I don't want Daisy to know I had him busted. I found out he has other outstandings. The court will put him away for a while. Daisy has nightmares about jail. I'd like her to think he just went away on his own."

"I'm not going to lie to her."

"You don't have to. The simple story is he just left. Stick with that. The truth is simple only if you leave out some details. Anyway, that's between her and me. I just wanted you to know the backstory. You can claim all the ignorance you choose."

Bolinas was getting old and Patrick didn't stay much longer. He hitchhiked north as far as Mendocino, then back to San Francisco. His previous house in the Haight no longer had room for him. He called Diane and crashed one night on a sofa at her parents' house in the Marina, where her father slipped a folded twenty-dollar bill beneath an end-table ashtray just to see if Patrick would steal it. He wasn't welcome there, even though he didn't take the bait. Diane passed him on to Helmut.

Helmut welcomed a playmate. He also lived with his parents, but it was a different situation—a big house in Pacific Heights, where Helmut had his own apartment above the garage. He even had a guest bedroom. Talk about a step above living in a garage. Helmut introduced Patrick to his parents as a visiting friend from school. He went to Stanford. Patrick never saw the parents again.

Helmut was a year or two older than Patrick. He was a big man, but not in a Charles Atlas way. He had the pear-shaped build of George Washington. He ridiculed athletes and avoided exercise, but he was not unhandsome. He had a rich boy's charm, that self-assurance. He was also a pothead. Instead of a cup of coffee in the morning to start the day, Helmut smoked a joint. He would light up anytime. His apartment smelled of marijuana and patchouli incense. His car ashtray was a nest of roaches. One of the reasons Helmut liked having Patrick around was that he didn't have to drive stoned.

Helmut was part of the San Francisco scene Patrick had ignored before, the music scene. It involved two things he had no interest in—psychedelics and rock and roll. They both were about losing control. He had no interest in losing control, of making a fool of himself. Control was one of the few things he still possessed. He went with Helmut to shows at the Avalon Ballroom and the Fillmore, with their acidhead lightshows and raw bands with names like the Dead, Big Brother, and Mothers of Invention. They were just loud to Patrick, and the crazed dancing crowds in the undulating lights, at first fascinating, quickly became threatening. So many people surrendering. Some nights, Helmut would disappear, and Patrick would drive his car back to Pacific Heights alone.

They went for road trips, sometimes with Diane, usually not. Helmut had other girlfriends. On overnight trips, like to Lake Tahoe or Big Sur, Helmut paid for the motel rooms, a green credit card. After a while, Patrick was doing all of the driving; he was becoming the chauffeur. Helmut was spending more time in the neighborhood near the park where Patrick had first stayed, Haight-Ashbury. Every week it seemed to be getting a little weirder, with Haight Street more like Telegraph Avenue, only with head shops and tie-dyed T-shirt vendors. Money was pouring from somewhere into this blue-collar neighborhood.

And people with money, like Helmut. Patrick was just his chauffeur, not his bodyguard. He would drop Helmut off—one of his other girlfriends lived there—but not accompany him. The Haight was not for Patrick—too many tattoos, too many zombies. Even more creepy than the acidhead smiles were the stares of the zonks trying to see through you into what they wished to see.

Patrick would take those opportunities to drive. It was a nice car, a German car, new. The San Francisco hills didn't bother it. There was no hot-dog steam table strapped to the roof. This was another mode of exploring. He was learning the turf. He even stopped at a gas station and bought a street map of the city and Bay Area. Maps were Patrick's kind of literature. Maps were the truth. No, maps weren't the truth, though they couldn't lie. The streets were the truth, the land. Maps were the indexes of that truth, the guides to bigger truths. Maps couldn't lie because they could always be checked against the actual, changed and verified. And the names on the maps were hints at the land's human history. There were many places more rewarding than the Haight, many vistas.

One day, Helmut asked Patrick to wait when he dropped him off in front of the old, closed Haight Theater. He thought they might be going for a drive. Half an hour later they were crossing the Golden Gate Bridge, headed to a small town called Sebastopol an hour north. This time they were not just touring; Helmut was on some sort of mission.

Helmut fired up a doobie, and they passed it back and forth. Helmut, unfortunately, sometimes got philosophical when he got stoned.

"We're under attack, man. Our generation, we're under attack. They're afraid of us, man, afraid of our freedom. The cops hate us. The feds hate us. Uncle Lyndon is trying to kill as many of us as quickly as he can over in Nam. It's a battle, man. They've drawn this line and said all of us on this side are the enemy—their own kids. We didn't choose it. We just want to be let be, live in peace and harmony. But that ain't America, man. This country always has to be at war, even with itself."

It was pretty country they were passing through rolling hills of green velvet with isolated farmsteads, horses inside fences. So much empty land—Patrick couldn't get used to it. So much space.

"Now it's open season on us college kids here at home." Helmut passed the joint, which was getting short.

"Don't you have a clip?" Patrick asked.

"Somewhere," Helmut said, and he finger-mined the ashtray.

Patrick turned down the joint. "How so?"

"How so what?" Helmut stopped searching and took a long final toke.

"How so, open season on college kids?"

"Don't you follow the news, man? Just two days ago, that Whitman dude in Austin shooting all those students from the university tower, just blazing away. Trained as a sniper in the Marines. Open season, man. And just two weeks before, that guy Speck taking out eight student nurses in Chicago. Not to mention all the peaceful protesters getting the shit beat out of them at demonstrations and all the weed busts. Open season. Next thing you know, there'll be a bounty on our ears."

"Where are we headed?" Patrick asked.

"Into unknown territory, man, an uncivil war."

"No, I meant today, in the car."

"I told 'em I'd check it out. Those cats don't like leaving their neighborhood. I got an address."

The address was in an industrial part of small-town Sebastopol, warehouses, body shops. Patrick had to stop at a gas station to get directions. It was hot in Sebastopol, inland, away from the ocean. Patrick was beginning to wonder if Helmut's secret mission wasn't involved with weed supply. He had heard that the good stuff came from these counties north of the city. The address was an old brick building with a loading dock. It looked unused. When Helmut got out of the car, Patrick stayed put. Whatever Helmut was up to, it was none of his business. Helmut didn't invite him along. The heat, the dope, the drive—Patrick reclined the driver's seat and took a nap.

The other car's arrival woke him. A man got out and went into the building. Patrick went back to his nap. The next time he woke up, Helmut was saying his name.

"Patrick, wake up. Come inside and check this out."

On their way to the building, Helmut added, "Look, I told them I brought you along for your expert opinion, so ask some questions that make it sound like you know what you're talking about. Try to get them down on the price."

It was a big old piece of intricate black machinery. Patrick had no idea what it was for. He was introduced to two men, who shook his hand. He was still waking up. He walked around the machine, pretending to inspect it, while trying to figure out what it was. There was a medallion that identified it as a Goss, but that didn't help any.

"Year?" Patrick asked.

The two men looked at each other and shrugged. "We've only had it since the *Courier Bugle* went down," one said.

Of course! A printing press. It was obvious now, those belts and gears, its open mouth. "Last time it ran?"

Shrugs again. "That would have been five years ago," one man said.

"Maybe more like seven or eight years," the other man said. "I don't think they used it to the end."

"Got the book on it?" Patrick asked.

'The what?"

"The original operations manual."

"I think so."

"Maybe."

Patrick squatted down to look beneath the machine. "There's something missing here, the other transverse carriage," he made up a term.

"No, no parts are missing."

"That we know of."

"Spare parts? Replacement rollers?"

"As is."

Patrick turned to Helmut. "Hard to get parts for this model. Hard to get someone who knows how to run it. At this age it will have chronic slippage problems."

"The price is negotiable," the second man said. "We need it out of here. It would be a shame to scrap it."

"Well, that's not my call to make," Helmut said. "The people I work for will get back to you. Thank you for your time."

Late lunch at a Mexican place in town. Margaritas. Helmut paid.

"What do you want with a newspaper printing press?" Patrick asked.

"Propaganda," Helmut said. "A counter-offensive."

Chapter 4

In Patrick's opinion, the *Oracle* never made it as propaganda. It wasn't even a manifesto. They did buy that press, but never got it running properly, too much a real-world hassle. Besides, they—Helmut's acidhead partners—decided they had to go with colors. Easier to job it out to some print shop that knew what they were doing. There was plenty of money; LSD sales were booming. There was an older guy named Larry, the longest greybeard, who claimed to know what he was doing and to whom everyone deferred when it came to technical stuff, but Larry had no say about content. It was hard to say who did.

Patrick was the youngest guy there, and they were all guys. His name was The Kid. At first, he hung around because Helmut was there. He had nothing else to do, and it was sort of interesting, the daily chaos. But then Helmut lost interest— "gang of space cases"—and left to go sailing in Baja. Patrick stayed on at Helmut's place, with the car. The parents were also gone on vacation, Germany, Helmut said. Patrick became sort of the gofer, the one person there who wasn't tripping or always stoned. It wasn't a job. He didn't get paid. He didn't know if anyone did. He was still collecting his unemployment check, though his weeks were running out.

They rushed out the first issue, just a dozen tabloid pages

and a total mess. In either tribute to or imitation of the Filmore light shows, the print pages were all overlain with amorphous shapes of colored tint screens, often at the expense of the legibility of the printed text beneath. What could be read was mainly dispatches from psychedelic voyages. The art work was bad Blake. What it looked like, what it said, meant nothing to Patrick. It didn't seem to mean much to anyone else either. The object itself, the ink and paper product, the vessel not its contents, was what mattered. There were no ads, and that first issue they gave away. The Kid got the job of standing on the corner of Haight and Ashbury and handing copies to whoever wanted one. The colored ink came off on his hands and shirt.

Having the car was freedom. Patrick continued exploring. Half Moon Bay, the Presidio, Mt. Tamalpais, so many places distinctly themselves. He never met anyone. He wasn't looking for people. The emptier the place, the better. It was early August, so the ocean fog would avalanche over the coastal hills, exchanging vast sunlit vistas for the nickel glow, the womblike isolation of just you and the road, always curving. He found a beach on Bonita Cove where no one else seemed to go.

On one trip north, he stopped in Bolinas. It was like a ghost town in the fog. He had a green death at nearly empty Smiley's, then drove up to Joanna's on the mesa. He had brought her books to return. Joanna was home, but she didn't want the books back. "I've got boxes of unsold copies," she said. She seemed happy to see him. "My current cabin dweller isn't any way near as helpful. It's nice having a guest on such a gloomy day." There were crutches beside her kitchen chair.

"What's with those?" Patrick asked.

In answer, she shifted in her chair and stuck out her right leg. There was a cast on her ankle and foot. Someone had painted flowers on it, daisies. "Done it myself, coming home in the dark."

"Is Daisy around. I wanted to say hello."

"She's about but out. I haven't seen nor heard her in a couple of hours. She has an unnatural fondness for prowling on days like this. You're staying in the city now?"

"Crashing at a new friend's."

"There's a lot going on there. Have you seen this new publication, the *Oracle*? What a presumptive name."

"Yes. My friend is involved with it. I help them out sometimes."

"I haven't seen it, only heard about it."

"It's pretty weird."

"So I've heard. Could you get me a copy? I'd like to see it."

There was a sound on the porch, and Patrick looked up to see Daisy peeking through the widow. She smiled when she saw him.

"Is that your car, Uncle Rick?" was the first thing Daisy said when she came in the door. "Super cool." She came over and gave him a hug. "Is it stolen?"

Daisy wanted to go for a ride. Joanna said she could use a few things from the grocery store in Stinson Beach, a slightly larger town five or six miles back on the coast road. Patrick and Daisy went for a ride. There was a state beach at Stinson, a real beach, long and white and wave-washed, not like Bolinas's small pockets of coarse sand. It was a tourist beach, day-trippers up from the city. But not this fog-bound afternoon. The short strip of shops along the Shoreline Highway was almost as deserted as Bolinas. Daisy wanted to go to the beach. The fog was colder there. The beach was deserted except for a man in a green army overcoat, walking slowly as he swept a metal detector back and forth in front of him.

"He's searching for things someone else lost," Daisy said. "That's sort of sad, isn't it?"

"Finders' keepers," Patrick said.

"That's what I mean—losers weepers. Someone else is weeping." They walked for a while. Solitary gulls watched them. "I don't want to be a loser." Daisy picked up a shell and threw it into the water. "And I don't want anything that someone else has lost."

The damp chill was getting to Patrick, and he turned to head back. Daisy threw more shells back where they'd come from. "My dad's in jail, you know."

"No, I didn't know."

"I thought mom told you when she let me come home."

He could claim what ignorance he cared, Joanna had told him. He said nothing.

"It's jail makes him act crazy. He used to be nice. You're not a writer are you, Uncle Rick?"

"Nope. Barely a reader."

"Dad's a writer. I think all writers are crazy."

"Your mom?"

"She's not a writer. She's a poet. That's different. But her friends who are writers are all…I don't know…not normal, not like other adults, creepy, in different ways."

"Oh?"

"Like that guy Greg who is in the cabin now. Boy, I wish you were still there. He smells, smells like he's never had a bath and he talks to himself, I mean like loud. I think he is reading what he's been writing, because it doesn't make much sense."

There was a coffee shop open, and before doing Joanna's shopping, they stopped in to warm up, a café au lait for Patrick and hot chocolate for Daisy, with two stale Danish pastries. Daisy didn't finish hers.

Patrick had taken to wearing some of Helmut's clothes, just a few sweaters and a leather jacket that didn't look too big on him. They were there, and Helmut wasn't. Patrick's backpacked wardrobe was limited and ill-suited to the damp chill of San Francisco's foggy August nights, and he liked the feeling of incognito. He had let his beard and moustache grow, hadn't shaved since leaving Manhattan. There was no reason to. It must have made him look older, because bartenders no longer carded him. He didn't drive Helmut's car at night. You don't prowl San Francisco in a car. From Helmut's place in Pacific Heights, it was just a hike downhill to North Beach and Chinatown, where he always began his evening's safaris, and from there to downtown and the Tenderloin. He avoided the Haight. On any given night he'd cover four or five miles. He'd stop in bars along the way, nursing an ale and watching the people. He would always end up back in North Beach before heading uphill to home.

During the day Patrick would stop by the *Oracle* offices above the shuttered Haight Theater. There was always stuff to be done. He did a lot of pickup and delivery. They were selling ad space now. There were a few women involved now, too. One of them, who called herself Sierra Sunshine, had taken a liking to Patrick. Those were her words— "I've taken a liking to you." Her husband called himself Editor-in-Priest. He and Larry greybeard had a lot of arguments, school-kid fights. Then, one afternoon, Larry stomped out, cursing the whole operation, and things exploded. Sierra Sunshine attacked Editor-in-Priest, and other staff and hangers-on took sides. It was sort of amusing, watching adults acting like high school kids. Editor-in-Priest started breaking things, then Sierra Sunshine and her clique threw him out.

That was the night Patrick finally lost his virginity, glad to be rid of it, something lost that no one else would ever find. Patrick had previously noticed that most of the folks in the *Oracle* crowd were like kids when it came to picking up after themselves. Cleaning up, even finishing things, was someone else's, some grown-up's, job. Everyone was too self-important to do menial things. Garbage had always been a problem. There were rats, as a result. He had even seen one of the artists walk away from a fire he had ignited in a trash basket with a cigarette butt. Picking up after them, taking out trash, breaking down boxes was part of what Patrick did there.

After the skirmish everyone left. The Editor-in-Priest's faction because he'd been vanquished; Larry greybeard's supporters because he had quit. "Bad vibes here, man," someone told him as they left. Patrick stayed behind because he belonged to neither camp. He was just The Kid. He cleaned up the Editor-in-Priest's mess—some overturned work tables, a smashed light-table, a kicked-over garbage can. He had nowhere else to go.

Sierra Sunshine had forgotten her purse and she came back for it. She was upset. She needed a ride. Patrick had Helmut's car. She needed a drink. They stopped at some bar she knew in the Sunset. She needed to go to the sea. He drove her to Ocean Beach. She wanted sushi. They went to Japan Town. She couldn't go home. He took her to Helmut's. As to the experience itself, Sierra Sunshine knew what she needed and took it. Patrick didn't mind; he didn't need what she took.

It was Sierra who told him about the chimpanzees. According to Sierra, the necessary interbreeding between chimp gene-pool populations was achieved by a few brave young males who undertook the perilous task of crossing the border from their native group to another. The males in the new group would beat the shit out of the pilgrim, trying to kill the interloper, but the ones strong enough to survive and recover would be allowed to stay and mate. She saw herself as Patrick's prize and welcoming committee of one. "I've never fucked a New Yorker before." She liked his young body, the fact that she could get him hard again. Patrick appreciated the fact that it was all hormonal, not emotional. Sierra stayed the night.

Word was that the former Editor-in-Priest was splitting town, taking his supporters north to a ranch in Mendocino and setting up an ashram, whatever that was. Larry greybeard came back, and the group reassembled. As a survivor, Patrick's position was slightly elevated. Now he was pretty much Sierra's gofer—not just anybody could ask him to do something. He still took out the trash, because no one else would. Sierra soon attached herself to a new in-house honcho, some poet who had published stuff elsewhere. With the Priest's departure any sense of a chain of command evaporated. Either everybody was in charge or nobody was, but the second issue was congealing, growing like something in a petri dish. One of the jobs no one wanted—it was tedious, unglamorous, and required concentration and a steady hand—was paste-up. Larry taught Patrick the basics and gave him the tools. It wasn't hard once he got the hang of it. It involved being neat.

The Haight was filling up. It wasn't just locals in the shops now. There was no place to park on Haight Street. There were more cop cars cruising and straights with cameras around their necks. Garish spray-painted graffiti started springing up like ugly urban flowers. The city was birthing a new sideshow. The tourists were coming to see the freaks. After watching the seals at Fisherman's Wharf, they'd stop by the human zoo in Haight-Ashbury. There weren't yet postcards for sale. An ice-cream parlor had opened to serve them.

One afternoon, a couple stopped Patrick on the sidewalk, he thought to ask directions. But no, the man wanted to know if he could take a photo of Patrick with his wife. Patrick had not had a haircut in months, not since shaving his head back in New York. He had gotten shaggy, and his still wispy facial hair had passed the phase of looking just unshaved. He was wearing Helmut's leather jacket. The wife came and put her arm around Patrick's waist and smiled at the camera. The man thanked him and gave him a dollar. He wanted to ask where they were from, but conversations were against zoo rules.

Patrick still had copies of the *Oracle's* first issue. He took one up to Joanna in Bolinas. She was off the crutches, with a walking cast and a cane. This time it was a hot, sunny day, the bank of fog lurking off the coast. He left the paper with Joanna and took Daisy for a ride to Stinson for ice cream cones. Daisy was sort of subdued. She could be that way. When she did speak, she talked about birds. She'd been watching them. She knew their names. As a New Yorker, Patrick knew pigeons and sparrows and gulls.

"Have you seen the movie, *Birdman of Alcatraz*?" Daisy asked.

"Nope, missed it."

"I haven't seen it either, but I heard about it. I was hoping you could tell me what it was about, what happens, how it ends."

"Sorry I can't help you out, Daisy. I don't see many movies."

"That's okay. Not important."

Stinson Beach was packed with day-trippers. They had to stand in line for their ice cream cones. They walked down to the beach to look at all the people in swimming suits.

"People are funny-looking, aren't they?" she said. There were no birds on the beach.

"They come in all shapes and sizes," Patrick said.

"Do you like girls with big boobs, like that one?"

"Daisy!"

"Just asking. I wonder how big my boobs will be."

"As big as they need to be."

Back on the mesa, Daisy took off with a pair of binoculars.

Joanna was miffed. "This rag is useless," she said. The *Oracle* was open on the table in front of her. "These people are interested only in themselves. Don't they know the country is flying apart?"

"I think their point is to ignore that."

"I had some hope for this. If I gave you something, could you get it published?"

"That's not exactly my role there. I sweep the floor."

"Your visit is quite fortuitous. While you and Daisy were gone, I got word that there's a happening in the city tomorrow that I ought to attend. Can you spend the night here and give me a ride in tomorrow?"

"I guess, but where? You got someone in the cabin."

"I got that someone out of the cabin. He wouldn't leave. I had to throw him out. Quesadillas for dinner."

The cabin had been trashed. After an hour of housecleaning the place still smelled. Some aromas are like an oil you can't wash away. One window was broken, a pane missing. There were half-burned papers in the pot-bellied stove. There was no bedding on the old mattress, which he flipped over. It wasn't his room at Helmut's. Funny thing about being on the road, how the meaning of home also becomes transient. Home is often the place you just left, rarely a place you'll return to. If you're without your pack, home is where you left it. If someone asks "Where's home?" you can say whatever you please. Home, if anywhere, is somewhere in the future.

Joanna came down carrying pillows, sheets, and blankets. "Had to wash these," she said. She left and came back with some incense sticks and a bottle of Old Forester.

"It's cold in here," she said. It was, a clammy breeze through the broken window. "And it stinks." She started lighting incense. "Why don't you light a fire?"

"There are some papers in there with writing on them. I didn't know if I should burn them."

"If they're in there, they're in there to burn," Joanna said, going over to the stove. "Oh." She laughed. "Those are Greg's rantings that I told him to destroy. He couldn't even start a proper fire."

Joanna had to go back up to the house to get a couple of glasses for the whiskey. She was gone a while. By the time she returned, Patrick had a proper fire going, a home fire burning.

"Had to read Daisy to sleep. I can't break her of that."

"What did you read her?"

"We visited Captain Nemo tonight. She has her shelf of favorites that she knows by heart. I know, because if I change anything, she corrects me." Joanna handed Patrick his glass of whiskey and sat down in the other ladderback chair by the stove. "What she wants to hear depends on her mood. She hasn't asked for Captain Nemo in a while."

The incense was nice. The heat from the stove was nice. The whiskey was nice. Was this what a home would be like? Nice things, familiar things, rooms you could navigate in the dark? More than three shirts to wear?

"Does Daisy seem changed to you?" Joanna asked.

"No, nothing unusual. This new thing for birds."

"Something's happened. I feel it."

"Something bad?"

"Something that changed her. Something she's hiding."

"She didn't like this guy Greg," Patrick said. Or was home where other peoples' problems and worries became yours?

"What did she say?"

"Only that he was smelly and creepy and loud."

"That's it. For the first time, Daisy feels vulnerable. I can't leave her alone just now."

Before Joanna went up to the house, she helped Patrick make the bed. Later, in the dark, he heard her play her piano concerto.

Chapter 5

Patrick didn't follow the news. What was the point? Whatever was going to happen was going to happen whether he knew about it or not. It was like weather forecasts, reading them had no effect on the weather. In a way, it was all propaganda—someone else's take on what was happening, what they want you to think important. Besides, if you followed something, didn't that mean you acknowledged it as a leader? Who wants to be led by the news? Helmut had called this attitude willful ignorance. But the world, the country at least, was badly fucked up. That was obvious. He suspected it always had been thus. He was nobody. Maybe the best he could do was avoid becoming a victim. It was like being on the road—the next destination was not the last; all choices had half-lives.

He had zero idea, for instance, who this Lenore woman was. She was in the news, a friend of Joanna's. He was supposed to know about her. Lenore was the reason Joanna was headed into San Francisco. She brought Daisy along. Patrick wasn't sure whether Daisy wanted to come or not. She wasn't sulking so much as subdued. Her hair wasn't up in a ponytail but down around her face, as if she was hiding. She brought her binoculars. She sat in the back.

There was a hitchhiker on the way out of town. Patrick had taken to picking up hitchhikers. It was a fraternal thing.

He started to slow down, then reconsidered—he already had two passengers. It was a young man, dressed all in black, including a black fedora.

"Oh, it's poor Billy," Joanna said, "Stop and give him a ride."

"Mom," Daisy said. It was a plea. Joanna ignored it.

Patrick was twenty yards past him by the time he pulled over. The figure in black did not turn around. Patrick tapped the horn. It took a while for Billy to get to the car. He walked with an old man's hitch, as if there was something wrong with one hip.

"Thanks. Tam Junction?" he said.

"Get in, Billy," Joanna said.

Daisy scrunched over as far as she could behind Patrick and looked out the window. There's a protocol to hitchhiking. First, you make no assumptions about the people who stop to pick you up. You are strangers, and it is best you remain so. Maybe they were looking for someone to talk to, probably not. There is no obligation for you to talk to them and vice-versa. In California picking up hitchhikers was more like a community service. You don't chat up your bus driver. They let you know how far they're going. You let them know how far you're going. No small talk, no chitchat. Billy seemed to have that part down. Even though both Joanna and Daisy seemed to know who Billy was, he evinced nothing reciprocal. His face was pasty pale. With his black clothes and black hat, he looked like a black-and-white photograph in the back seat. Daisy ignored him, looked out her window. Joanna had nothing to say. At first, the silence was uncomfortable, then it wasn't.

Patrick preferred rides in the backs of pickup trucks,

where he could avoid the whole thing and just toss his pack into the back and follow it, get up against the cab out of the wind, and watch where he was coming from. That was always easiest, best, the least contact.

Patrick took the coastal route, the ocean vistas rather than the forest tunnels. There was always less traffic. Helmut's car liked the curves. It was almost like a nature amusement-park ride, with sudden death just off the right shoulder. It wasn't until they were headed inland down to Muir Beach that Joanna spoke up.

"Billy, heard anything from your dad?"

"No. Tangiers." It was almost a boy's voice.

He got out at Tam Junction.

"Do you need for anything, Billy?" Joanna asked.

"No."

As they drove off toward the bridge entry, Joanna said, "Sorry if that bummed you out, Daisy, but I feel so sorry for that boy."

"He's the creepiest," Daisy said, still looking out her window.

"If you saw your father shoot me through the head, you'd be a little creepy, too."

"The father who is now in Tangiers?" Patrick asked.

"It was an accident. They were playing William Tell with a pistol. She had a water pitcher on her head. His father was drunk. It was in Mexico."

"He's sick," Daisy said.

"I'm afraid he's taken after his father. Drugs and alcohol. He's only in his twenties and already on his second liver."

"His father is a writer. He's crazy and creepy," Daisy

said. "Uncle Rick, can we stop for a hot dog someplace? I'm hungry."

The traffic was backed up on Columbus and on Broadway, clogged by cars, crowds, and cops. While they were stuck in traffic, Joanna explained why they were there. There was a protest rally—she called it a rally, like it was a sporting event—at a bookstore in North Beach. A week before a clerk there had been busted by an undercover cop— "Pigs in a blanket," Daisy said and laughed—for selling him a book.

"Lenore's dirty book," Daisy said. "Mom didn't like it either."

"No, I said it was better than her earlier work. I just thought its explicitness was cheap. She was just trying to get it busted. I mean, six pages with a lot of words you're not supposed to put in print."

"Mom wouldn't let me read it," Daisy said.

"Anyway, she succeeded, and her *Love Book*, as she called it—just a pamphlet, really—got a clerk busted and her in the headlines."

"And this?" Patrick asked. Some asshole was honking at him as he tried to switch lanes and find a side street.

"A community gathering to express their displeasure at fascist censorship."

Patrick made a right onto Vallejo.

"Look, let us out here. You're getting farther away. I didn't know it would be like this."

Off to their left there was the pop of shells being fired and, shortly after, puffs of tear gas fog drifted with the bay breeze over rooftops.

Joanna got out. "Come on," she said to Daisy.

"How will you get back?" Patrick asked.

"Not your worry. Come on, Daisy, let's go."

Daisy hadn't moved. "Nah, I think I'll stay with Uncle Rick."

"I...," was all Joanna said as she locked eyes with her daughter.

Patrick opened the glove compartment and pulled out the pad and pen Helmut kept there for recording his stoned insights. He wrote down Helmut's address and phone number. "You can find us here," he said, handing Joanna the torn-off page. "Be careful."

Patrick didn't feel like hot dogs, so they had pizza at a place on Union Street instead. Daisy took the pepperoni off her slice and put it on Patrick's. Patrick was having trouble matching what Joanna had told him with what he had just glimpsed happening. A bookstore clerk had gotten busted for selling a slim book of poems, which resulted in a riot? There was a lack of proportion there. Why bust a book of porno poems, in a city famous for its strip clubs and laissez-faire morality? Why bring tear gas to a bookstore protest? Daisy didn't care. She wanted to go to the zoo.

"They have birds there, don't they?"

Indeed, they did have birds, beautiful birds in tall aviaries. This was Patrick's first zoo visit, not just to the San Francisco Zoo, any zoo. The New York zoo was way off in the Bronx. Of course, he was sorry for all the prisoners. Who wouldn't be? Daisy was happy. She came out of her shell. It was her first zoo visit, too. And it wasn't just the birds. Her second favorite attraction was the building with all the snakes and crocodiles and turtles, where nothing moved.

"They seem to like it here, don't you think?" The pacing big cats gave her the heebie geebies. "I dislike all cats. They kill birds for no reason. Mom doesn't like cats either. We agree on that, but I wouldn't mind having a dog. Do you think she'll be alright?"

"I trust your mom to take care of herself."

"I dunno. She likes the spotlight, you know. Uncle Rick, what was that white smoke?"

"That was tear gas, I believe."

"Why is it called that?"

"I guess because it makes you cry."

"They want to make people cry?"

The police seemed to want to make a lot of people cry these days, especially the anti-war crowds and the blacks. They had used a lot of tear gas in Harlem two summers before, during that protest, and, of course, every peace parade and anti-draft rally deserved a good dose. Gas attacks were outlawed in war, but it was okay to gas your own citizens, even over a bunch of impolite words that everyone knew and used every day. Go figure.

"I guess it's better than shooting them," Patrick said.

"Mom thinks she's bulletproof."

When they got to Helmut's, Daisy surprised Patrick by promptly curling up on the couch and going to sleep. Helmut had a TV, and Patrick turned it on. Would they have coverage so soon? Would they interrupt regular programming, or would he have to wait for the five-o'clock news? Was it even newsworthy enough to cover? He turned the sound all the way down.

When the five-o'clock news did come on, it opened with shots of police in riot gear and fire trucks and clouds of what looked more like real smoke than tear gas. The volume was still off and Daisy was still asleep. When he turned the sound up, Daisy woke up and sat on the edge of the couch, staring at the screen. Could this be where they had left Joanna? This war zone? The buildings looked different. It took a few minutes before the announcer informed them that these were scenes from the day's events in a place called Watts in Los Angeles. Whatever had happened at the North Beach confrontation didn't make the news. L.A. was on fire, a "race riot" they called it, as if that was all the explanation needed.

When Joanna arrived, she wanted to get stoned. "Watts?" she asked.

"We saw it on the news," Patrick said.

They watched it again, updated at eleven. Daisy watched it, too, silently, Joanna's arm around her on the couch. There really was nothing to say. All Joanna said was, "It's all cascading." She and Daisy went to sleep on his bed. Patrick went for a long hike down through the Tenderloin, where nothing had changed—junkies and pushers and prostitutes, the smell of urine.

A few days later, Helmut showed up at the *Oracle* office. Patrick was trying his hand at ad paste-up, trickier stuff. He was surprised to see Helmut. Patrick had grown accustomed to his absence. Helmut was equally surprised to find Patrick still there, still living in his apartment, still driving his car. He had forgotten him also. For some reason, he thought Patrick was long gone. Helmut's confusion was greater than Patrick's, but he quickly got over it. Nothing seemed amiss with his car or his apartment. In fact, Helmut noted that his house plants looked happier and that the kitchen was cleaner and had lost its old smell.

Helmut would be returning to campus early, in a week or so. He had some make-up work to do from the spring semester. His parents were still in Germany, but they were returning. When Helmut left, Patrick would have to leave, too. Patrick had been thinking about the draft. He had had a 2-S deferment before he dropped out of City College. Maybe they would take him back, night school. He could find a day job. Last time, he had tried taking day classes and working a night job, but that didn't work out; he got no sleep. City College was free, just fees and books. If he took enough courses, he could get his deferment back. His unemployment was about to run out.

Patrick was at odds with himself about the 2-S deferment. Why should some guy lucky enough to get to go to college also be exempt from becoming a military slave? It was like a fixed lottery—only winners get to win. On the other hand, personally, he had no desire to face a future as a federal felon draft evader. That might cause problems down the line. But he had a few more weeks to decide. Meanwhile, Helmut's return altered his day-to-day. He no longer owned the car. He still went down to the *Oracle* office. It was just a short hike down Divisadero. Larry had come to rely on him. Everyone else was irregular.

A couple days later, Slim, of all people, showed up at the *Oracle*. He was looking for Patrick. He had an envelope from Joanna for him. Slim scowled at everything, including Patrick. Inside the envelope was a note and a poem. The note told Patrick to get the poem into the next issue of *Oracle*. The poem was about things on fire—buildings, books, ideas, Vietnamese villages, children's minds—and, once again, about denial. Patrick had no idea if the poem was good or not. He didn't have the tools or confidence to judge. He slipped it into the manila folder of copy Larry had asked him to take to their typesetter. He marked it up as he had seen Larry mark things up for title display type and text type. Other pieces like this Larry often had set in Italic; Patrick called for Italic. Then he changed it to bold Italic. It might as well stand out. He'd find a place for it in paste-up. Joanna's name was also in bold.

Larry's bust halted everything. He was set up—a bogus police raid searching for weapons and the "accidental" discovery of a bindle of cocaine in Larry's desk drawer. Larry didn't drink or do drugs. Everybody knew that. He was AA. The cops had gotten a mole into the *Oracle's* hangers-on, a woman named Francine, whom no one liked but no one suspected, she seemed so always out of it. Who knew she carried a badge? She had probably planted the coke. The cops were there when Patrick walked down to work. He just kept walking. He got the skinny later from Helmut, who still had connections in the Haight. His girlfriend there was pregnant.

Diane and Patrick had gotten together now and then over the summer, at first with Helmut, then more often not. She was into the music scene, but she didn't like going to shows alone. Sometimes she'd call Patrick to see if he wanted to be her body guard. She had moved out of her parents', who were getting a divorce she wanted nothing to do with. She had taken a room in Cow Hollow, just down the hill from Helmut's. Occasionally, Patrick would stop by, and they'd go out for something to eat or a drink on Union Street. He'd listen to her problems. She missed New York. She couldn't go back to school before the dorms opened. Her mother was drinking too much. Her allowance wasn't big enough. She hated Dylan going electric. Why didn't Patrick shave and get a haircut? She did like to walk, and they went for some hikes through the Presidio. When he had to leave Helmut's, she said he could crash at her place for the few days before she flew back to New York. They slept together in her queen-sized bed.

Patrick had decided to go back. There was nothing left to hold him in California. He hitchhiked up to Bolinas to say goodbye to Joanna and Daisy, leaving his pack at Diane's. He would miss all this open space. He would even miss the fog. He reported to Joanna that he had snuck her poem into the next *Oracle* issue, but he was not sure when or even if it would be out. She now wanted the poem back so she could change it, but there was nothing he could do about that. She was displeased. Daisy walked with him down to the store on his way out of town, and he bought her a fudgesicle. She wanted his address.

"You're my only uncle," she said. "What if I decide to run away to New York. How would I find you?"

Patrick's only mailing address was care of his sister's post office box in Chelsea. He wrote it down for her. "Let me hear from you," he said. "Drop me a line now and then with your news. I'll write back. I promise."

There were no vehicles leaving Bolinas. He walked all the way to Stinson before catching a ride. It had started to rain. In all his months in the Bay Area it had rarely rained. It was a cold rain, relentless and bored. Another long wait with his thumb out at Tam Junction. It was like he'd become invisible. He wondered if it was the beard. That night, in Diane's bathroom, he shaved it off. Diane approved. She thought he did it for her.

The day before he decided to leave, he picked up and cashed his last unemployment check, then stopped by Helmut's. He still had a set of his house keys. He thought he would just leave them in the mailbox with a thank-you note, but Helmut was home. His car was in the driveway. His pregnant girlfriend was there with him. Helmut was different around her, nervous, unsure of himself. Along with the house keys, Patrick gave Helmut his New York mailing address. "Let me know if you're coming to my town, so I can return the favor of your hospitality," he said.

Chapter 6

Patrick was on the road before dawn. For no reason other than he had the time—a week before he had to be back in New York—he headed north, not east. He had already crossed America on the boring intermittent Interstate. He had liked what he'd seen of the coast country north of San Francisco. He'd see more of it, then head across the Trans-Canada highway, new country. He had kept the sleeping bag and ensolite pad Naomi had loaned him. He wouldn't have to spend money on a room when he stopped. It meant an extra thousand miles or so. It felt good to be heading out. Every departure is an escape.

Something very strange had happened in the night. He had been almost asleep when Diane, beside him in bed, began trembling. She was fetally curled with the blankets pulled over her head—a soft, halting, fearful moan. Patrick didn't feel he knew Diane well enough to ask. He waited for her to say something, to include him in whatever it was. He sat up. The room was dark except for a window's faint city sky glow. Her trembling became more pronounced. She crawled deeper under the covers.

"What is it?" she whispered. "Whose is it?"

"What?" Patrick asked.

"Is it yours or mine?"

Patrick stared into the dark. Diane moved up against

him, one arm across his bare rib cage. It wasn't a shape. It was a gathering of slightly lighter air just off the foot of the bed. Patrick glanced at the window. Nothing had changed there. When he looked back, the paleness was stronger, more condensed. Diane stiffened, buried her face in the side of his chest. There was a vague shape now, a figure, tall and broad shouldered, like anthropomorphized fog. Diane's nails dug into his ribs.

"What do you want?" Patrick asked. "You are scaring the woman."

For a few seconds the fog brightened, then it slowly vanished. An aroma lingered behind, an old, familiar but unnamable, not unpleasant woodland musk. Patrick could feel the blood running down his side from where Diane's nails were embedded in him.

Afterwards, Diane did not want to talk about it. Patrick only asked once. She slowly relaxed, at first into a nearly catatonic state, then into denial. There was nothing to explain, because nothing had happened. Patrick went to the bathroom to tend to his wounds and wash up. When he came back out, he had decided to leave. The inexplicable is best left behind. He started to dress.

"You're leaving?" Diane asked.

"Early start."

"For the best. And you can take your specters with you."

Packing was quick because he had never unpacked. Diane took two of her sleeping pills. As he left, she said, "Make sure the door is locked behind you." Patrick was sure of one thing—that whatever it was that had just happened, it had nothing to do with him. It belonged to Diane.

Quick but short rides north through California. With a purple marker Patrick had made a sign on a folded brown supermarket bag. He spelled Vancouver wrong, leaving out the "u" so it would fit. A couple of people picked him up just to point out his mistake. Stupid meant safe. But in Oregon, the rides came further apart. As dusk approached, he was mid-nowhere in a forest, and it was drizzling. Traffic was thin. Maybe this heading north wasn't such a good idea. He had a plastic poncho to keep him and his pack dry, but that wouldn't help much if he had to sleep in the rain.

The truck that stopped for him already had its headlights on, a logger headed home. He took pity on Patrick and took him to his house. That night Patrick had dinner with the logger's family. The kids made fun of Patrick's long hair. After dinner, the logger, a big, broad-shouldered man with hands the size of bear paws, had beers with Patrick at the kitchen table and asked about what was going on in San Francisco. Patrick was shown a space in the hall to spread his pad and sleeping bag, and in the morning, after breakfast, the logger took him to a spot on the highway where he could continue north. "Good luck."

It was over five hundred miles from Bend to Vancouver, but thanks to a couple of big booster rides he made it past Seattle in good time, where he lucked out again and caught a ride with a guy going all the way to Vancouver. He'd be there by nightfall. Maybe he'd splurge on a cheap motel room and a hot shower. The driver was chatty. Patrick had to say very little. He didn't even have to listen much. At the border, a uniformed officer asked the driver if he was Canadian. The car had British Columbia plates.

"Yep, going home to Burnaby."

"And your friend here?"

"Don't rightly know. Just picked him up down the road for company."

They both looked at Patrick. "No, American," Patrick said.

"American" was not the right answer. Patrick was asked to get out of the car. His only identification was his driver's license and expired City College student ID card.

"Another draft dodger," the uniform said. "Get your pack." Then, to the driver, "You can go." He turned and went back to his control booth. Patrick stood there. There was no one else around, no other cars going in either direction. The sun was at the top of the trees. The guard looked back at him and pointed down the road. Patrick put on his pack and left.

It was chilly in the woods, a damp chill. It had to be ten miles back to the nearest town. Shit, he was just a city boy. What was he doing, getting himself stranded in the north woods? In any event, he was not going back. He'd come this far. He hid in the forest until it was full dark, then he headed back along the margin of the trees toward the border. There had been a big open field to the right of the border guard station. He'd head across there, giving the guardhouse a wide berth. Maybe there was a fence, but how far into the woods could it go?

There may have been a moon behind the clouds, but there was no natural light in that field, just the faint umbra of the distant highway lights at the station. Slow going on uneven ground. Then, in front of him, a gathering greyness in the air, something that wasn't black appearing. What, again? He stopped. The shape shifted, floating toward him.

He half expected it to speak.

It neighed. The light far behind him reflected off an eyeball above him. Then the pale head of a horse emerged not three feet in front of his face. Patrick could smell him now. He said hello. He took this as proof that he didn't have to believe in ghosts.

He crossed out of the field and into more forest. There was no border fence. As he found his way, he concentrated on heading straight, heading north. He came to a road and followed it east away from the border crossing. When he saw headlights, he ducked back into the trees. When another road cut off to his left, he took it, putting distance between himself and the border. He walked all night. There were farms and crossroads. He kept heading north and east. At dawn, he found a secluded spot to spread out his pad and sleeping bag. He had never been out of the U.S. before. All he could feel was exhaustion.

The rest of his trip across Canada was a painful blur, a trek. He would never repeat it and would recommend it only to an enemy he had not yet met. The best he could say was that the authorities—where there were any—ignored him. At least half of his encounters with locals were unpleasant, including some of his rides. At one forlorn Saskatchewan crossroads he was stuck overnight. At Winnipeg, he gave it up and headed south to North Dakota.

At the U.S. border, they couldn't keep him out, but they could hassle him. They had him empty his backpack and spread its contents out on the macadam. They didn't like his long hair and the fact that he didn't have a draft card. One of the uniforms had a son in Nam and didn't hide that he considered Patrick one of the enemy. It took three more days to reach Manhattan, his final ride in a New Jersey farm truck delivering vegetables to the city. The driver asked Patrick to give him a blow job. He took no offense at Patrick's refusal. He went to his sister's in Chelsea. He had left clothes and stuff there. It was just a one-bedroom, but she would let him crash till he found a place. She had a new boyfriend who disliked the arrangement.

They let him back in to City College, but only as an evening-school student. Exaggerating his experience at the *Oracle,* he landed a minimum-wage job doing paste-up for a local shoppers' rag. To get him out of her hair, his sister loaned him the deposit on a walk-up studio apartment in Spanish Harlem. Back to all the closed spaces of New York—classrooms, work cubicle, one-room pad—and the subway cars connecting them. Routines exist to camouflage the humdrum. He took a class in American Lit, the next semester Shakespeare's tragedies. He moved up from the shoppers' rag to a porno mag and got an apartment on the Lower East Side. He stayed in night school. His sister married that jerk.

Every so often, Patrick would get a letter from Daisy. He watched her age—her handwriting, her choice of topics, her jokes. For some reason she thought every letter should have a joke or two. He learned about her getting a dog, Toby, and of Toby's mysterious demise—her term. She reported her mother's protest arrests like a court reporter. Big dictionary words started to appear. She asked if he'd read *Catcher in the Rye,* calling him Uncle Holden. Patrick always wrote back. One year she mentioned her birthday party, and every year after that he sent her a birthday card. There were gaps, and then there would be a spate of exchanges. She started signing her letters with different names, as if she were auditioning them.

There may have been no tuition at City College, but there were student fees and there were textbooks. Because it was free, most of the students were poor, especially the night-school students, many of whom, like Patrick, worked menial daytime jobs just to survive in New York. Textbooks were expensive. If you were taking four courses, one semester's bookstore bite could be a month or two's rent. Bookstore theft was pandemic. Patrick was a practitioner. He made no attempt to justify it. It wasn't a revolutionary act of anti-capitalist defiance. He wasn't "liberating" the books; he was stealing them, because otherwise he could not get them. It was theft, plain and simple. He was good at it. He had done it every semester he'd been there.

At the beginning of his senior year, he got caught. The college had hired moonlighting NYPD detectives to try and staunch the bookstore's hemorrhaging. The new policy was immediate expulsion if you got caught. The cop was good, an inconspicuous black dude dressed like any other student. Patrick got pinched with two books tucked in his belt beneath his sweater. Patrick was handcuffed and marched to the night-school dean's office, where he was to surrender his student ID and get thrown out before being taken to the precinct for booking.

The dean, a woman, pulled out a form and started to fill it in. Patrick tried to get comfortable in his straight-back chair with his hands cuffed behind his back.

"Detective, have you read your suspect his rights?"

"Yes, ma'am."

"Then, would you mind waiting outside while I conduct this interview? This part is institutional, not criminal."

"I need to get him booked, ma'am."

"Yes, of course, in due time. Just a few minutes." She looked at Patrick's ID card, then at him. "And you can remove the handcuffs. They're not necessary here. Are they, Patrick?"

The officer didn't want to, but he did. She started to fill in the blanks on the form. The cop had put the evidence, the books he had found on Patrick, on her desk—a paperback on sampling theory and Genet's *The Thief's Journal.* Patrick saw her smile at the Genet.

"Required reading," he said.

"Professor Jordan's class?" She wrote down the prices of the books. "Have you stolen any other books from the bookstore?"

"Yes, of course."

She looked up at him. She was neither old nor young, attractive nor unattractive. A silk scarf was tied around her neck. "Often?"

"Every semester. They're required. How else do I get to read them?"

"Could you estimate their total price?" Her pen hovered over the form.

"I could estimate, but it would take some time."

She looked again at his ID card. "Is this your senior year, Patrick?"

"Yes. It was."

"You do realize this means you will be immediately

expelled."

"Yes, and that the officer is doing his job and you are doing yours."

"And that you will be losing your student deferment and will probably be drafted? They seem to be drafting anyone eligible these days."

You don't get to be dean without a command of the obvious. He nodded.

"Can you make restitution?"

"For these two, yes, I guess. For the rest? No way." Patrick rubbed his wrists, returning feeling to his fingers.

She took off the glasses he hadn't noticed she was wearing.

"Could you give me a list—an estimate—of all the books you have stolen and their net worth?"

"I could try."

"And could you write me an essay explaining your… your situation and what brought you to stealing those books?"

"I guess so, sure."

The dean put down her glasses and pen and went to the door. "Officer, you can return to your station now. You can leave him with me. Our institutional procedures are not complete. You have his information. We will inform you when you may proceed with your processing when we press charges."

"That's not the deal, ma'am. I caught him in the commission of a crime. I take him in."

"You do excellent work, officer. I will write a commendation. Thank you." She shut the door. The dean set Patrick a deadline. He had twenty-four hours to compile an inventory of his bookstore thefts and to write a detailed description of his motivations and methods, typed, double-spaced, to be delivered to her tomorrow, same time, same place. In the interim she would temporarily stay his expulsion and arrest. He could go.

When he left, the policeman was waiting by the exit. "You lucked out this time, white boy. If I see you again, I'm taking you right in. No honky mama apron strings. If you were a brother, you'd be busted."

Patrick made her deadline. He called in sick to work and devoted the day to the task. He was rather proud of his essay, "The Crime of Poverty," which he had rewritten and expanded several times. She told him to return the next day. In the end, the incident report form and his theft tally were placed in a sealed envelope in his file. If he got in trouble, any trouble, again before graduation, he would be immediately expelled. At the start of the spring semester, he stole what books he needed from the Columbia bookstore.

The spring semester never ended. The City College campus was in Harlem, well, on the expanding edge of it, and it was built like a red brick fortress. The spring before, the campus had been shut down during the riots that followed Dr. King's assassination. In '69 everything was coming to a boil. Anti-war protests were happening on campuses across the country. Helicopters were gassing students at People's Park in Berkeley. The Students for a Democratic Society was taking over the peace movement. The summer would bring Woodstock and the Stonewall riots in Manhattan, and more protests. At City College, civil rights and anti-war demonstrators shut the campus down, with the protesters inside the campus walls and the police outside in a standoff.

Patrick had to sneak inside the campus, climbing a wall to drop off his final papers. There would be no graduation ceremonies, no celebrations. There was no cause to celebrate, no commencement, only an ending. In the midst of a society collapsing, succumbing to its own pathologies, the degree he had completed seemed meaningless. There was no reward beyond ending a task he had set for himself, one ending lost amid many, including his draft deferment. He never received a diploma. There was no going forward into the chaos, only waiting it out, surviving.

Patrick had a job now he didn't mind doing, making deliveries for an upscale liquor store on the Upper East Side. Highrise cliental, good tippers. He got to double-park a classic black step van with Italic gold lettering. He declined the uniform. Sometimes he was hired by his regular customers to come back in the evening to bartend their cocktail parties. He'd overhear the guests' comments about peaceniks and hippies and the niggers. The wives would flirt with him. He was always the last to leave, after cleaning up.

1976

Chapter 7

Patrick had never seen the city from above before. Approaching SFO, his flight flew high over the bay, out to sea, then circled back from the south as it descended. From his portside window he could see it all in the setting sun—the bay, Oakland and Berkeley, the packed peninsula surrounded by blue, and beyond that the green mountains of Marin with its thin blood-rust thread of connecting bridge. There were more tall buildings downtown, casting long shadow fingers toward the bay. It had been ten years, but he was back. It was an unofficial part of the divorce—she got the East Coast; he got the West Coast. Neither cared about the middle.

In the end, it had been surprisingly easy to leave New York. As he discarded things she hadn't taken, a forgotten sense of freedom had returned. For years he had lived in fear of change. Then, after all the legal stuff was done, he felt again the thrill of departure. He had to leave the magazine because she worked there, too, as did her new lover. But that was a plus. He'd been stuck there, nowhere to go. There was a parallel job in L.A., but he turned it down. When the job in S.F. opened up, something different, he jumped on it. The money was good. Going back was like returning to an old girlfriend.

San Francisco had changed, not radically, but incrementally. It was no longer the blue-collar city he remembered. The docks had died with the war. Suits had moved in. Rents had gone up. If most of the city was still middle-class and below, the well-off seemed more obvious, flaunting it. The Haight was dead, a sad tour-bus ghetto of burned-out freaks. It took Patrick a week to find a furnished, dingy one-bedroom on Russian Hill. He didn't especially like the place or the décor, and it was too expensive, but like everything else in his life now, it felt temporary. He could walk to work. The streets of the city still felt the same.

Patrick's new job was as production manager of in-house publications for a large corporation with headquarters in the Financial District. It wasn't a particularly challenging job, but what he did was a mystery to his bosses, so they overpaid him just as they overpaid themselves. He had a staff of five who knew what they were doing. Patrick had to buy a couple of new suits so that he could look just like the rest of middle management. His boss was a vice president; his suits were more expensive. Patrick wasn't clear on exactly what the corporation did, but that wasn't necessary. His job was to get copy and art work designed, printed, and bound. It could be in Japanese as far as he was concerned. There were a lot of graphs, but nothing complicated. The big job was the annual report. He was told to spare no expense on that.

Although Patrick had a driver's license, he had never owned a car. You didn't want one in Manhattan. His New Yorker wife had never learned to drive. He had no need for a car in San Francisco either. If he wanted to get out of the city, he would do what he did in New York, rent one. It took several weeks for him to settle in and get used to the city. One sunny Saturday he rented a compact and headed north, across the Golden Gate. Not much seemed to have changed in Marin. He stopped in Sausalito, just off the bridge, and had lunch. There was a juggler at the ferry dock, juggling bowling balls for the tourists. Across the sparkling bay, the San Francisco skyline looked like Oz.

Bolinas hadn't changed much either, a little less shabby perhaps. Smiley's had a fresh coat of whitewash. It was crowded. Joanna was home. The house hadn't changed, but her hair was now all white. She remembered him, "Uncle Rick." Daisy was in college now, at Mills in Oakland. Only she wasn't Daisy any more. She was Meredith. She had seceded from Bolinas and her mother.

"I'm afraid she's gone over to the other side. To see what it's like," Joanna said.

"Mills is pretty costly," Patrick said.

"Oh, she got a scholarship. And her father's got the bucks, sold a novel to Hollywood, lives there now. Looks like you're not a hobo any more either." Joanna got up to put the tea kettle on and came back with a pipe of ganja. They got stoned and drank green tea with honey. It was like a conversation interrupted by a decade.

Patrick's wife—he would not use her name, trying to forget it—didn't smoke or drink or use drugs, and she had objected to Patrick doing so. Except for wine with dinner, he hadn't found it hard to give them up. So, it had been five years since he'd gotten high. He had forgotten the euphoria of letting everything go. Joanna extracted truths from him. Not just her brow but her whole face furrowed when he talked about New York. For some reason, he told her about the ghost who had seen him off when he left San Francisco.

"I know that ghost," she said. "He's harmless."

As if on cue—ah, the coincidences that seem meaningful when you're high—the fog arrived on a breeze that jangled the many chimes on Joanna's porch, a memory sound as clear as déjà vu. Joanna asked and listened. She made observations but gave no advice. They laughed often. She still had the practice of reaching out and touching his arm or the back of his hand when she said something personal. When Patrick asked, she told him about Toby's mysterious demise. "She never mentioned the case of the stolen heifer?"

Joanna fixed rice and spicy black beans. They shared another pipe. "Caution, this new stuff is sneaky." She played cuts from an Emmylou Harris LP she wanted him to hear. "Not just listen to, but hear." The new stuff was sneaky. Patrick knew he couldn't drive the twisty road back in the fog and the dark. He ended up crashing in his old cabin, which hadn't changed.

Patrick's boss, Douglas, was not like the other vice presidents, of whom there seemed to be many, none of whom were female as far as Patrick could tell. Douglas was only a few years older than Patrick, but they came from different worlds. Douglas was South Carolina, money, Duke, an un-New York urbanity. His suits were French. He wore a mustache long enough to twirl. There was a dart board on a wall of his office. They both had a tendency to work late, when there was no one there to bother them. They might see each other getting coffee or at the Xerox machine, but their nods and greetings were purely office politesse. They weren't there to chat. Then one evening, they ended up on the same elevator as they left, and Douglas suggested they stop for a drink. There was a bistro around the corner. Douglas drank Pernod. Patrick had an ale. They ended up having dinner in Chinatown.

After that, they often ended their extended work days together with drinks and darts in Douglas's office, followed by dinner somewhere, more drinks. Douglas was new to the city as well, only recently promoted from the Phoenix office. He was single, divorced. He also knew no one here. It was through Douglas that Patrick met cocaine.

Cooking for one was a thankless task in a city with so many good restaurants. Patrick's kitchen was near totally bare. Sometimes he would bring home take-out. But why eat shitty processed food when within walking distance was a world of cuisines? After a while he had his favorite noodle shops and steakhouses and Italian ristorantes. With Douglas his culinary horizons broadened. Douglas was a fan of Asian food, not just Chinese and Japanese, but Thai and Vietnamese, Indian and Korean, Filipino and Mongolian. On a typical evening they would do a few lines of blow in his office, then head out to find a new place to eat. Chopstick exploring, Douglas called it. The places were spread out all over the city, but Douglas had a car, still with Arizona plates, and with Patrick navigating by street map they'd search them out in neighborhoods they otherwise would never have visited.

One after-work evening, as they were playing darts in Douglas's office, a temblor hit. They were on the 18th floor. The jolt wasn't bad, but the building started to sway. The dartboard was moving back and forth. An ashtray slid off the desk, and an open bottle of Anchor Steam toppled. Douglas turned white and grabbed the back of a chair. It was his first earthquake. It totally unnerved him, vanquished all his casual swank. It stopped, of course, as they always do. Time started up again. A swig from a fifth of Stoli in a bottom drawer, a white worm up his nose from the mirror on his desk calmed him a bit. Patrick cleaned up the spilt beer.

"We don't allow those where I come from," Douglas said.

"No, just hurricanes."

"How many people died in the '06 quake?" Douglas asked. His hands were still shaking.

"Don't know. That was seventy years ago; they'd all be dead by now anyway."

There were sirens now, far away and below them, as if from another time, either past or future. There was a smaller after-jolt.

"Should we leave or should we stay?" There was panic in Douglas's voice.

"We can see if the elevators are still working."

That evening Patrick learned about Douglas's fear of death. Douglas knew it was excessive, beyond what others felt about it—though he couldn't understand that. They were back in that bistro where Douglas drank only Pernod. He was trying to recoup by confessing. He wanted Patrick to forgive his seeming cowardice. The phobia had been there as long as he could remember, beyond his control—the nightmares, the terrors. As a child, he had never had pets because he knew they would die. His parents had him in therapy for it, then the therapist died. He had seen other shrinks since, to no avail. "There's no pill for it, no cure." His marriage had ended when his wife said in passing that she'd like to kill him for something.

Patrick learned more than he wanted to know. The bistro was packed with folks happy to be alive. Nothing had changed, nothing was broken. All the sirens were off in the distance.

"I think you're taking it too personally," Patrick said.

"Is there anything more personal than dying? How can you live without dread of it ending? Like that. For no reason."

Back in New York, it was the summer of the Son of Sam murders, young women dying for no reason. In San Francisco, it was the Patty Hearst trial. Across the country, it was the bicentennial year. It seemed to Patrick that the celebrations all felt obligatory, the country making an effort to put on a fake smile. They had just lost a war and fifty-five thousand troops, for no reason. The populace seemed more fragmented than ever. Real civility had vanished. This all felt appropriate and in need of being ignored. Cocaine helped.

San Francisco was awash with it; maybe "adrift with it" was more descriptive. Bolivian snow was everywhere. Stoli and blow fueled the night life. The empty white paper bindles it came in were common litter in men's rooms. Women's rooms, too, probably. Pairs of partyers would disappear into lavatories and exit laughing. Patrick only snorted other people's coke, mainly Douglas's. It was a learned high; you had to open the door to it. But it was worth repeating. Patrick thought of it as a sharpener. Douglas was funnier coked up, in his Southern Colonel character, his slow drawl and disarming charm like a matador's cape hiding the blade of his cruel wit.

Crisp new twenty-dollar bills were a part of the cocaine culture, both for purchasing and for inhaling it—a rolled-up double-sawbuck being the preferred cool instrument. Douglas thought it providential that concurrent with the drug's explosion on the scene was the recent introduction of automatic teller machines that dispensed only crisp new twenty-dollar bills. Thus far, there were just a few such machines, on the outside of banks, accessible 24/7. Douglas knew where they were. After dark there were usually lines. Women referred to snorting a line as powdering Andrew Jackson's nose.

There were plenty of women in the club scene. Women's Lib was real. Freedom was almost an obligation, independence a duty. Patrick found them entertaining, but he had no interest in engagement. It was as if that part of him had been amputated. Douglas also had no interest in "chasing tail," as he put it. "It will take me a while to get that stupid again," he said. The women assumed they were a gay couple. That was not unnatural in San Francisco. They were almost always together.

The gay scene was its own separate cocaine cotillion, out in the Castro and some leather bars in the Western Addition, not their crowd. For some reason, the city had become an American Homo Mecca. Patrick heard about that scene from his designer, Rex. There was no shortage of gay men and women in the publishing biz, even in New York, but here in San Francisco they were more out about it. Rex certainly was. He was a good raconteur. One of the copy editors, Marna, was a proud lesbian, and she and Rex would gossip and banter. Rex claimed to be jealous of Patrick—and he probably was—because he knew Patrick and Douglas were friends, and he had a crush on Douglas. It was like a soap-opera plot that he and Marna had worked up as ongoing office entertainment. "Gays of Our Lives." Douglas knew nothing about it.

Douglas didn't like walking. He collected parking tickets instead. He said they were in his budget, curb rent. So Patrick still had his solitary evening city strolls. It was his only exercise. There was nothing to keep him in his dreary apartment. North Beach was his favorite destination. The mix—locals and out-of-towners, beatniks and businessmen, Italians and Chinese, limos and beggars, bookstores and bars, strip joints and Washington Square. It was the part of the city most like Manhattan. One night he strolled up an alley off Columbus across from the City Lights bookstore. There was a bar he hadn't noticed before. It hadn't been there in '66. A small sign called it a museum.

Patrick's first impression was that there should have been swinging western saloon doors at the entrance. Not that the place looked like a saloon from a cowboy movie, but that he had just passed through a time gap into a pub from another, a better era. No TVs, no juke box, no games, no pool table, no bright lights or neon beer signs. A long, low-ceilinged room, with wooden tables and chairs and a mirror-backed bar along one side, walls covered with an antique-show collection of photos and posters and objects. The soft roll of many conversations. Most of the chairs and barstools were occupied. These were all locals, no suits or frocks. There was nothing here for tourists. There was only one window, in the front out onto the alley, with a deep, waist-high sill, like an empty window seat. Patrick went there.

There were almost as many women as men at the bar, and, except for one guy reading a book, everyone seemed engaged in conversation. Two women were talking with the bartender, a large bearded man who had them laughing. On the bar in front of some of the men, along with their cigarettes and ashtray, were tall cans of Rainier Ale. Patrick had forgotten green death. Douglas would not appreciate the nickname. When the bartender noticed him and came to the end of the bar for his order, Patrick asked for a green death. A woman at the bar handed it back to him with a smile and a nod and a look that lingered. For the first time in more months than he cared to count Patrick had a twinge of feeling at home. The Irish flag was pinned to the ceiling above the bar. The bartender's name was Liam, from Dublin.

The place was known as Specs, after its proprietor. On subsequent evenings, Patrick met Specs and learned the names of other regulars, older folks mainly, what the tourists would have called beatniks. A casual crowd of professional drinkers and talkers, leftists in politics, not sports fans, smokers. Joints were shared, in the alleyway. There were no empty cocaine bindles on the men's room floor. His evenings at Specs were the inverse of his club-tour nights with Douglas—mellow, rather than frenetic. People had things to say, and you didn't have to yell to be heard.

Patrick had never had a neighborhood bar like his dad

had had in New York. Specs became his neighborhood bar. It was only nine or ten blocks downhill from his place. One night he complained about his apartment, and Deborah, one of the barmaids, said, "Well, let's find you new digs." It was that kind of place. There was a community bulletin board where you could post anything. There was a shoebox on the bar filled with postcards from travelling regulars reporting back from Paris and London, Buenos Aires and Tangiers. He met a woman there named Petronella who drew a sketch of him on a cocktail napkin and added her phone number.

One day Patrick received a letter forwarded from his old address in New York. It was from Meredith, nee Daisy.

Dear Uncle Rick,

I heard from mother that you had moved back to the Bay Area.

Of course, she had no idea how to reach you. This is the last address I have for you, your last letter from years ago that I never responded to.

I still have it. I hope this finds you.

Mother said she told you I was at Mills, just across the Bay.

Let's get together, if you like. I would. For old times' sake. Also, I have something of yours to return to you—a belt with a bison-head buckle I stole from your pack as a keepsake the day you left.

Meredith

No telephone number, just a return address on the envelope, a P.O. Box at Mills College.

Chapter 8

Maybe Oakland didn't deserve its reputation, maybe it did. The inherent comparison to its classy and famous neighbor across the bay didn't help any, the ugly sister syndrome. Its motto could be Stein's "There's no there there." It was known as a place to escape from. In the national news it was the Black Panther Party, crime, and civil unrest. If you lived in San Francisco, it was a place you didn't visit, just the other end of the Bay Bridge and a bunch of freeway exits as you headed east to Tahoe. It was like Queens to a Manhattanite. But there were several Oaklands, and basically the demographics changed with altitude, the distance from the bay—the higher you lived, the higher your income bracket.

Mills College was up the hill, a campus of many trees and confusing roads. It was a women's college whose tuition was pegged to Stanford's. Academe as gated arcadia. Meredith had said she would wait for Patrick on the steps of Mills Hall. He only had to find it. For some reason—he couldn't name it—Patrick had rented a pricier car, a sedan rather than a compact. He asked for a black one. Something about his destination? He wouldn't have recognized her. The younger you are, the more a decade can change you. She got up from the steps and walked to the curb even before he pulled up. She was as tall as her mom but of sturdier build, broad-shouldered, hair that hadn't yet lost all its childhood blond.

He buzzed down the passenger-side window, and she stooped down to look in. "Why, if it isn't Uncle Rick in his rental rickshaw."

"At your service, ma'am."

She was carrying a small bouquet of randomly plucked flowers. She passed them through the window toward him. "I stole these for you," she said.

"How public-service-minded of you. Get in."

They had a late lunch at a seafood place she picked out down in Jack London Square, overlooking an arm of the bay. Patrick was careful not to call her Daisy. It wasn't that hard; she was no longer Daisy. She wasn't quite a Meredith yet either, but closing in on it. She had brought his belt with the bison-head buckle to return, which he recognized but couldn't remember missing.

"No, you keep it," he said, turning her theft into a gift. "I don't think it would suit me anymore."

Like a good uncle, he quizzed her about school. Like a good niece, she was evasive if positive. She was a junior, majoring in something called media studies; or maybe she made that up, because she laughed when she said it. Her laugh was still Daisyesque. He gave her a brief account of his transition from being a paste-up man at a porno mag to a production manager at Conde Nast. She was interested in New York and the publishing biz. He did not mention his marriage or divorce.

"Mom said you had a wife who left you. Why haven't you mentioned that?"

"I haven't asked you about your boyfriends, have I?"

"That's because you don't want to know. But I do. What

was she like? Was she American? I pictured you in New York with an exotic woman."

"Nondisparagement clause in the divorce. Legally bound not to discuss her, but no, she was not exotic." She was definitely not exotic, rather the opposite. If Meredith was going to get personal, so could he. "How are things with you and your mom?"

"Mom wanted me out of there." Meredith paused to extract meat from a lobster claw. "I wasn't a particularly cooperative teenager." Another pause as she dipped it in the drawn butter and ate it. "You know, I had to go over the hill every day to go to high school in Mill Valley. I started not returning home after school. She had me arrested once."

"Your scholarship?"

"Lucked out there. Partly because we're so poor, and then mom did a reading at Mills and got to somebody. I guess they liked the idea of helping out the famous lady poet's kid. It's not totally free, by the way. My dad pays the fees."

On the way back to campus, Meredith had Patrick stop at a convenience store. She came out with a box of Kotex in a plastic bag and a packet of Reese's Peanut Butter Cups for Patrick. "Are these still your favorites?" she asked. They were. She gave him directions to her dorm.

"Let's do this again," Patrick said.

"Absolutely. The food here is sincerely mediocre."

"You've got my number."

"And you mine." She leaned over and gave him a kiss on the cheek. "My favorite uncle."

"I thought I was your only uncle."

"That too." Meredith got out of the car, then leaned back

to the window. "You know, my mom is kind of lonely these days. A bunch of her friends have either died or otherwise left, and she's made enemies of others. She likes you. I think maybe the New York connection. Anyway, stop up and see her now and then. I worry about her. Too much time alone and she can get a little crazy."

Patrick found his way off campus and onto MacArthur Blvd. downhill. His sun-wilted flowers were still on the dashboard, up under the windshield. He left them there when he returned the car.

There was one other reason for going to Oakland—baseball. The A's played there. Patrick was a baseball fan. He really didn't care about or follow any other sport. When he left New York, he had to leave his Mets behind. *Mets* always takes the personal possessive pronoun. He had been one with them since their inception in '62 and through all those early awful seasons when he was a teenager. He would get out to Shea Stadium for home games as often as he could afford it. The last few years he had had a season ticket. Just one season ticket. The non-exotic wife held the sport—all sports—in contempt and thought Patrick—all sports fans—ludicrously plebeian. His seat above the third-base line had been his escape.

He had always taken the subway to Shea. Now, he could take the BART train to the Oakland Coliseum. There was a team closer to home, the Giants, playing down at Candlestick Park, but Patrick adopted the A's. Candlestick was a miserable cold place to be a fan, and the Coliseum, though farther away, was easier to get to. And the A's were not the

Giants. Patrick had been raised to despise the Giants after they deserted New York. Of course, there was also reason to dislike the Athletics, who had defeated the Mets in the World Series just three years before. But he admired their pitching and the brand of open, spirited game they played. They reminded him of the Miracle Mets of '69.

Now there was a season, Seaver et al, that could never be beaten. The Mets climbing out of the cellar of their early years and taking the pennant, then the Series, over the Orioles. Patrick especially cherished one weekend that August at Shea when the Mets swept the Padres in twin double-headers. Patrick was there for the Sunday games and just knew that the sweep meant the pennant. It was the same weekend that everyone else his age would later claim they were upstate at Woodstock. He was proud he was at Shea instead.

He still went to ballgames alone. He preferred it that way, just him and the game, anonymous in a friendly crowd. One of the endearing comforts of a ballgame is that everybody knows their role. The players, of course—the skilled and graceful entertainers, highly trained and muscle-memoried, their on-field demeanor prescribed by generations of protocol tradition. The umpires (not judges or referees, but arbitrators) with their own set of dance steps and symbolic gestures. The fans, each alone but united in their attention. They know why they are there, so that for the space of several hours they can park the burden of their life's concerns outside the gates of this green park and just be a fan. The beer and the peanut vendors know their roles and calls. The peace from being part of an unconscious ceremony.

The A's played in the other, the American, League. So

Patrick was in somewhat unfamiliar waters—the new designated-hitter rule and some truly funky uniforms. The White Sox played in shorts. He managed to catch some night games. Then the A's had a weekend homestand, with day games on Saturday and Sunday. Seeing as he was going to be in Oakland, he called Meredith to see if she was free for dinner either night after the game. It never occurred to him to invite her to the game. Women didn't like baseball, didn't get it. That was cool; Patrick didn't get ballet.

Meredith was busy Saturday, but Sunday she was free. When Patrick said he wasn't sure what time he would pick her up because it depended how long the game lasted, she asked, what game? She wanted to go to the game. She had never been.

There was something wrong from the start. This was a different Meredith than the one of their previous date. That edgy-energy, post-Daisy had been smoothed out like ironed-away wrinkles and replaced by a casual sophisticate in sunglasses. She even spoke slower. No nosegay of pilfered flowers. She hadn't brought a purse the first time; this time she sported a colorful woven Mexican shoulder bag. She gave Patrick a kiss on the cheek—lip gloss—when she got in the rental car, again a black sedan. She relaxed into a pose as they drove away from her dorm. This was a new scenario. They were no longer Uncle Rick and Daisy.

It was a perfect baseball afternoon. They got seats in the sun down the right-field line. The groundskeepers were smoothing out and hosing down the infield dirt. The umpires were gathering behind home plate. Meredith was chitchatting, nothing personal or important. She hooked her arm into Patrick's as they strolled to their section. The closer she got to him, the further away he felt. Who was this young woman on his arm? What role was she playing? Who was he supposed to be?

By the bottom of the fifth, Meredith had had two beers. She wasn't old enough to drink legally, but this was the ballpark, and, technically, they were his beers. He had bought them. Her speech was even slower now. She showed little interest in what was happening on the field. It was a dull pitchers' duel; only one run had scored. She was sunning herself. She had taken off the light tan jacket she was wearing, beneath which was just a tangerine tank top. It was like she was posing again—the picture of pulchritude. The young man on the other side of her was enjoying the show. Patrick was not enjoying the game. At least she was not asking a lot of questions, like she used to when she was Daisy. Patrick despised the designated-hitter rule. It was undemocratic.

Twice Patrick saw Meredith rummage through her bag for a little silver pill box, then take a pill. He thought little of it. Women and their pills. His ex had had endless menstrual cramps and was always popping pills. In the seventh, the A's finally put some hits together, men on second and third with no outs. Meredith had to go to the ladies. She needed Patrick to take her. She took her jacket and bag. He heard the roar as they entered the tunnel. Meredith wavered as she walked and held onto Patrick's arm. He waited for her at the exit from the ladies. He could tell from the crowd noise that the A's rally continued. She came out the entrance to the ladies, looking around for him.

"Sorry to take you away from your game, but can we leave?"

"Are you okay?" She still seemed a little unsteady.

They walked toward the exit ramp.

"The beers," she said, "the sun, the boredom."

"And the pills?"

"Yes, the pills. I probably shouldn't take them when I drink."

They were on the curving, descending ramp. She was using the railing.

"What are the pills?"

"Different pills for different thrills, nothing illegal like you smoke and snort."

"Where do you get them?"

"They're everywhere. I was at a party last night where there was a punchbowl on the table filled with all kinds of uppers and downers, all different shapes and colors, like jelly beans, take what you want."

"Pharma roulette."

"Why don't you take me back to the dorm? I don't think I would be a very good dinner date. I'll take a rain check. That's a baseball term, isn't it?"

The A's won, four to one.

One plus of the new job was the absence of aesthetes. At Condé Nast too many staffers had pretended that they really weren't trolls but undiscovered authors or artists awaiting their ascendancy. At the corporation, the sole measures of worth were the level of your compensation and the size of your office. These were MBAs and card-carrying capitalists for whom the code word for intellectual was nerd. They were easier to deal with. Even Rex, the sole artist on Patrick's crew, saw himself as a technician, rather than a Titian, in spite of all the amphetamine he inhaled off his light table.

Patrick quickly came to rely on Rex. He had been on the crew longest, through several bosses. He was the institutional memory. He knew which suppliers would miss their deadlines and by how much, so that Patrick could build proper pillows into his scheduling. He knew which department heads were assholes and how to deal with them. He knew all the dirt, all the gossip. He ordered the office supplies and dealt with the bicycle messenger services they relied on. On Patrick's birthday—he hadn't mentioned it to anyone; he wasn't acknowledging it this year—Rex surprised him with a cake and a small office party, inviting Douglas.

Patrick came to appreciate that Rex's smooth systems management owed much to a sub-rosa gay network that operated in the trade like a cooperative triad of favors. Rex's connections made Patrick's job easier. Afraid to lose him, Patrick arranged for Rex to get a raise. Douglas was amenable. Rex was thankful. He invited Patrick to dinner at his house. "Home cooking," he said, "or rather, casa cooking. Raul will fix us a true Mexican meal. He wants to meet you."

Raul was Rex's housemate. Their house was in Bernal Heights, a part of the city Patrick didn't know. He took a cab. The cab driver didn't want to go there. Patrick had to give him an extra five. He wasn't sure what to bring to a Mexican meal, so he brought a bottle of tequila. It was sort of a third-world neighborhood above the Mission District, with wonderful views of a distant first-world metropolis.

From the outside, their house on a steep street was just like its neighbors', a cheap battered prewar bungalow. There was nothing charming about the block. Charm costs money. Rex's place did have new windows and a front door that belonged in a better neighborhood. When Patrick pushed the doorbell button, a dog barked twice. Only, it wasn't a real dog; it was the sound of a dog barking twice instead of a bell. He pushed the button again, the same two barks.

Rex welcomed the bottle of tequila, and Patrick met Raul, who came from the kitchen, wiping his hands on a dish towel. He looked just like a big Desi Arnaz, pompadour and all. The house's interior was in a state of reconstruction. All non-supporting walls had been ripped out. The ceiling was bare beams. The floor plan was totally open. Only the kitchen looked finished, with new appliances and cabinets.

"We've only been in here a year," Rex said, "and we're taking our time with the remodeling because it's so much fun." Raul laughed from the kitchen.

The meal was ideal. Patrick had no idea chili rellenos were supposed to taste like that. Tecate and tequila. Two more men joined them after dinner, one of whom was named Richard. A pipe was passed several times in the course of the evening, but Patrick figured it was the tequila that turned the pleasure knob to high. He had never drunk tequila before. The conversation flowed and bounced around. Rex put on a Frank Sinatra LP. Raul followed it with Freddie Fender. Richard requested Judy Garland, but was voted down. The ease of it all, the infectious laughter. The absence of women.

That was it. Without women around, men act differently. The gender tension was gone. Aside from Judy Garland, no woman had entered the conversation. A whole set of behavior protocols could be ignored, and you could relax. It was loosening your tie and unbuttoning your collar. It was like taking off your shoes. There was a reason why men everywhere and in every era have formed fraternal societies. It was why in many indigenous cultures the adult male population gathered together and slept in communal males-only lodges, while the women and children had their own commune. Comfort. It was why men created rites of passage and initiation ceremonies, why they shared tattoos and invented cults of masculinity. Jesus and his gang of twelve amigos. By nature, males belonged in squads of their fellows. Procreation was one thing. The company of your mates is quite another. There were so many answers in tequila.

When it came time to leave, Patrick asked Raul if he would call him a cab.

"They won't come up here, not this time of night. You can crash here."

"No, thanks. I need some fresh air. I'm not tired."

"I'll walk you down to BART."

"No need. I can find it, I'm sure—downhill, somewhere on Mission Street. Twenty-fourth Street Station?"

"Nah, it's not safe alone. Some tough streets between here and there."

There was a cold breeze off the bay. Patrick zippered up his jacket. They headed downhill. "What about you, coming back up the hill, alone?"

"No one mess with me. I'm a brother." He padded his coat pocket. "And I got protection."

Chapter 9

Of course, there are people who can tell one cow from another, but to city boy Patrick they were all just cows. Some had horns, others udders. Then there were species like Canada Geese that even the most obsessive admirer could not tell one from another. Was there any species that displayed as much diversity in appearance as homo sapiens? Just in the subset of so-called Caucasians in the Bay Area there was a vast array of shapes and shades and peculiarities. Douglas liked nude beaches. One Saturday, Patrick went with him to one at a private lake up in Marin. It was a scorcher June day. The place was crowded. It was more a pond than a lake, surrounded by sloping lawns, and no one was in the water. The lawns were filled with naked homo sapiens sunning themselves. Was it a sun cult or a skin cult? An exhibitionists' union. There were many perfectly tanned—no pale bits—bodies, but no two were identical. Patrick was the palest nude there.

That was the only time Patrick went nude sunbathing with Douglas, but he had discovered the quiet comfort of it. He didn't need the crowd; there was little voyeuristic about it. If everyone is naked, nudity is nothing special. But there was a childlike freedom in shedding your clothes and letting all your skin enjoy the sun and air. He remembered a beach he had found ten years before, exploring the Marin coast, where he had seen a few nude sunbathers.

The next weekend was another hot one. He rented a car and crossed the Golden Gate. The fog bank was waiting, like a snow-covered ridgeline, a mile or two out at sea. The turn-off was just past Sausalito. The beach was inside the national park recreation area, a hike in from the gate where you had to park. The hike was what made the beach special. It wasn't a place you casually visited. It wasn't much of a beach, either, a wave-pounded cove hemmed in by cliffs.

There had been other cars in the car park, and there were other people on the beach, none of them sunbathing. What Patrick remembered was a smaller pocket beach around the corner of the southern rocky point. If you timed it right between waves, you could make it round the point without getting drenched. He removed his shoes and socks and rolled up his pants legs, waited, watched the waves, and made a safe dash for it. There, in the sun, behind the sand berm windbreak were four solitary naked sunbathers, stretched out on blankets, reading. He joined them, finding a place to settle and strip as equidistant from each of them as he could get. They each made a point of ignoring him. He had brought his own reading material, but it didn't take. He kept rereading the same page. He didn't want to escape where he was. He watched the gulls. He listened to the waves on the other side of the berm. He studied the unclimbable cliffs around him. His mind wandered, free to meditate.

His meditations must have passed over to sleep, because someone was waking him, a hand on his shoulder. "Hey, wake up. Time to go, stranger." It was one of the other sunbathers, the woman with sun-streaked hair, now fully dressed, her daypack on her back. "Tide's coming in. If you don't get out now, you won't." She waited for him as he quickly dressed and packed up. She looked away as he got dressed, embarrassed by his loss of nudity. They both got wet as they went around the point. Her name was Candice. They hiked out together, and he gave her a ride back to the city, dropping her off in the Marina District, near where Diane's parents had lived. He remembered the house. It hadn't changed.

Oakland again. It wasn't Patrick's kind of event—a poetry reading—but there he was, at an art gallery on San Pablo, sitting on a folding chair, drinking warm Chablis from a plastic cup. He had been brought there by Deborah, the barmaid from Specs. One of the bar regulars was reading, and Deborah had organized a support field trip, though in the end there were only four of them came over on BART. Patrick felt he owed it to Deborah, who was still searching for a new apartment for him. The reading was late starting. Their poet, Larry, was there, but there were two other poets on the program, and they had not yet arrived. No one seemed especially concerned. Patrick was surprised to see that one of the other poets was Joanna.

Larry was drunk, or something. Deborah found him a cup of coffee and took him off somewhere. The gallery was full of large canvases, some of which had been moved aside to make space for the audience's chairs and a podium. The paintings were obviously all from a one-person show—no two were unalike. They were all featureless soft pastels. They looked spray-painted. All Patrick could surmise was that they were depictions of the sky on a very peaceful day. That lighter patch there might be the fog drifting in. If you owned one, would you mount it on your ceiling? They were like six by eight feet. The place filled up. Maybe it was the free wine.

Were poems supposed to be like crossword puzzles? Patrick never did get it. Why not just say what you have to say? Joanna's poems were better. At least her sentences made some sort of sense; you just had to guess how they fit together and what it might mean. The two male readers—Larry and some dude on speed named Howard—seemed enamored by how lost they were in what they were reading, as if they were sharing an unsolvable mystery. Patrick spent most of the reading standing at the rear of the audience by the table with the jugs of cheap Chablis. He had to hand it to them. It took guts.

At the end, the poets signed and sold some of their books. Larry finally fell over, knocking down one of the over-sized canvasses, which fell onto another, starting a domino effect that had the pleasant potential of flooring many more before someone stopped it. In the confusion that followed, Joanna ended up leaving with Patrick and the Specs contingent, minus Larry, on the walk to the BART station and the train back to the city. She accompanied them to Specs. Deborah was impressed that Patrick and Joanna seemed to be such old friends. On the train they sat together.

"It being in Oakland and all, I thought maybe Meredith would show," Patrick said.

"She learned to dislike such events as a child," Joanna said. "I doubt she even knew, much less cared about the reading."

"I didn't know about it, that you were reading, I mean. I was dragged there for Larry's sake."

"Poor sot. His early stuff was really quite good—spare, understated. Then someone gave him a drink and told him he'd been making too much sense."

They didn't stay long at Specs, but headed uphill to Patrick's place. Joanna was worn out. The couch in his living room unfolded into a bed, and he offered it to her. They had a nightcap when they got there. Patrick mentioned that he had twice met up with Meredith.

"Yes, she told me about your first date. Lobster. But I haven't heard from her since. Another dinner date?"

"An A's game, actually. I don't believe she enjoyed it."

"How did she seem? It's been months since I've seen her."

"She's a college kid."

"Of course. What an evasive answer."

"She's trying things out. She'll be alright. Pretty, smart, in a good space."

"From evasive to vague. Forget it. It's pointless to worry about her, but I do."

Patrick unfolded the couch and brought a pillow and the blanket from his bed. He had no extra sheets. Joanna crashed, and soon after, so did Patrick.

He was awakened sometime later by Joanna pushing on his back. "Move over. I can't sleep on that piece of shit mattress." She had brought her pillow and the blanket. Patrick was thankful for the blanket back. He'd been cold without it. Joanna added extra warmth beneath it. It had been a long time since he had shared a bed with anyone. She was a peaceful sleeper.

Douglas did not like the term "aplomb" applied to himself. "Sort of fruity, isn't it? What do you mean? Makes me think of someone overweight and haughty. Is that supposed to be a compliment?"

"Okay. Composure. Is that better?" Patrick said. "Just commenting. Yes, a compliment."

They were on Interstate 280, heading north back to the city. They had driven down to Sunnyvale for a meeting with one of Patrick's suppliers, a printer with whom he was having contractual hassles. Douglas had come along to loan some corporate muscle, and the ride. That had been hours before. They had had drinks after the meeting and then searched out a Korean restaurant Douglas wanted to try in Palo Alto, followed by a Bolivian-fueled university pub crawl. It was almost midnight now by Douglas's dashboard clock.

"I mean, their lawyer had nothing to counter your confidence."

"They can't afford to lose our account," Douglas said. "I could have been wrong. It didn't make any difference in the end. Find a new printer anyway." Douglas was doing ninety in the outside lane. There was very little traffic going into San Francisco at that time of night.

No, aplomb was the right coloration. It wasn't just confidence. It was the assumption of infallibility. It was what Douglas wore like an aftershave, his superior air of rich white-boy privilege. He knew how to use it. He had no reason to question it. Nothing and no one had ever caused him to question that this was his world. He may have a death phobia, but nothing in life had ever challenged his inherent sense of superiority. His attitude about parking tickets, for instance. His disdain for rearview mirrors.

The trooper got close before hitting his siren and lights. Douglas looked miffed. He took his time changing lanes and pulling off onto the shoulder. He looked bored as he buzzed down his window and got out his wallet. He gestured for Patrick to look in the glove compartment for the registration. When the trooper came to the window, Douglas handed him his driver's license without being asked and without saying a word.

"Would you step out of the car, please." Patrick couldn't see the officer's face, only as high as his badge.

"Why? What for?" Douglas asked.

"Just step out of the car, sir."

Douglas sighed and got out. His silence was haughty. When the officer asked him to turn around and put his hands on top of the car, Douglas sighed again and complied, shaking his head at this foolishness. He was frisked and then asked to put his hands behind his back.

At this Douglas spoke up. "What do you think you are doing, officer? A speeding ticket?"

"You're coming with me. Not just excessive speed and an expired out-of-state license, but there's a warrant out for your arrest, several actually—contempt of court for unpaid fines." He took handcuffed Douglas back to the patrol car and put him in the caged back seat. Then he returned to Douglas's car. Patrick was still sitting there with the registration in his hand.

"ID please." He took Patrick's New York driver's license back to the patrol car. When he returned, he handed Patrick his license back and asked if he was fit enough to drive. The keys were still in the ignition. In fact, the car was still running. "Drive safely."

The rest of the night did not improve for Douglas. At the police station he was given a breathalyzer test and failed. The forgotten remains of a bindle of coke was found in his shirt pocket. Douglas also discovered that being locked in a small holding cell could trigger one of his thanatophobia panic attacks. A company lawyer had him out on bail the next day. It turned out that the corporation had a lawyer whose specialty was springing their executives from just such embarrassing situations—part of the cost of doing business in San Francisco. Two days later, Douglas was back at work, and the only person there—aside from his bosses—who knew of his arrest was Patrick. And the bosses didn't know that Patrick knew. At work, Douglas hadn't changed. Perhaps he seemed a bit more aloof.

Patrick's home phone never rang. He wondered sometimes why he had it. No one ever called. No one, except for Meredith, even knew the number. It wasn't in the phone book yet. So, when the sound of it ringing and ringing and ringing worked its way into his dream and then woke him in the middle of the night, he figured it had to be a wrong number. It stopped, but now he was awake and had to get up to take a piss. He was doing so when it started ringing again and kept ringing. This time he answered it, just to let the caller know it was the wrong number, probably off by just a single digit. It was 2:30 a.m. Maybe a drunk.

It was Meredith. She didn't apologize for calling him at such an odd hour. There were no polite niceties at all.

She needed help, 400 dollars. She didn't say for what, just "Don't ask," and he didn't. "I can't talk now," she said. They arranged to meet at his office in the morning. "Give me time to get to the bank," Patrick said.

It was eleven before Meredith got there. "I've never seen you in a suit before. Nice office." She went to the window, where, between other office towers, you could see a slice of the bay and the Marin end of the Golden Gate. "Nice view."

"Are you in trouble, Meredith?"

"You said you wouldn't ask."

"I said I wouldn't ask what the money was for. Are you in trouble is a different question."

"Dad's having one of his hissy fits. I can't promise I'll pay you back. You've got a nice tan. Been on vacation somewhere?"

"School's been out for weeks now. You still in the dorm?"

"Moved in with a friend for the summer."

"In Oakland?" Patrick had her cash, in twenties, in an envelope. He held it out to her.

"No, here in the city. Thanks."

"How long do your dad's hissy fits usually last?"

"You're just full of questions, Uncle Rick. I won't ask you again," she said, sticking the envelope into the back pocket of her jeans. "Have you been up to see mom?"

"No, but I caught a reading of hers in Oakland. She hadn't heard from you."

"She doesn't want to hear from me. She never likes the news."

Douglas knocked on the door after he opened it. He was looking at the papers in his hand as he came in. "Patrick, Hausman has done it again." Then he saw Meredith standing there. "Oh, sorry. I didn't know you were…." He smiled at Meredith. "Hello, I'm Douglas."

Meredith smiled back at him. "Good for you. That's okay. I was just leaving. Thank you, Uncle Rick."

"Wait, Meredith. I don't have your new number."

She told him a phone number. Patrick wrote it down, then read it back to her. "Right?"

"Right. Nice meeting you, Douglas."

Douglas watched her leave. "Your niece? You never mentioned having a niece here."

"What about Hausman?"

"Now he wants that spread by the end of the month." Douglas handed Patrick the papers he was holding.

"What do you pay that advertising agency for? This is their job."

"Yeah, but it gets charged to his budget if I have them do it. Meredith? She's cute."

"She's too young for you, Douglas. Just a college kid. I'll have Rex drop what he's on and do this. You could try doing a favor for us now and then instead of just doing favors for everyone else."

Douglas was writing something on his palm. "All in the loving corporate family, bro."

The next time Patrick went to his secret beach, Candice was there. It was a chillier day. The onshore wind was blowing sand off the top of their protective berm. The fog bank was just offshore. A few other people made it around the point, but they didn't linger. There were no gulls to watch, just a pair of darker, stiff-winged birds stalled in the wind above them. Only one protected corner of the beach was possible for sunbathing, and they both ended up there. It was different with a woman you knew by name and had seen with clothes on. It turned a solitary pastime into a shared one. Now they weren't just naked; they were naked together. Now the sight of her breasts with their slightly aroused and raised nipples attracted him. Now when she lay on her back, he could see the lips beneath her pubic bush. She had to have noticed his thickening member. The fog won the beach, and they dressed and headed out. This time they stopped at the No Name in Sausalito for Irish coffees. They exchanged phone numbers. She gave him a peck on the cheek when he dropped her off.

Chapter 10

The whole thing was Candice's idea. For some reason, Patrick went along. He was not a camper, but Candice knew of this perfect place.... The Fourth of July was on Monday, so they would have the long weekend. She would bring all the gear and supplies they would need. She could borrow her housemate's backpack and sleeping bag for Patrick to use. All he had to supply was the rental car and himself and the clothes to wear coming and going.

They set off before dawn on Saturday, headed across the Golden Gate and then north on the inland route toward Ukiah. It was only a couple hours' drive. Patrick followed Candice's directions onto a mountain road along a stream until they came to a clearing where a few other cars and campers were parked. From there it was backpacks and hiking up a well-trod trail along the stream bank. The sun was barely up. The canyon was still in shadow. It was fresh and cool in the forest. They came to a spot where the stream spilled over a series of low falls into a broad pool whose banks were scattered with small tents and nudists. A soft breeze brought the scent of mosquito repellent.

Their arrival garnered some attention, but Candice, who was in the lead, walked right through the encampment with nods to those watching them. Farther up the stream a smaller creek came in from the right, and they picked their way up its rocky bed. She chose as their campsite a small clearing by the creek. It looked pristine. The sun was now breaking in splotches through the high canopy. They cleared a space big enough for the two-person tent Candice had brought and for a campfire. She erected the tent, and they brought rocks up from the stream for a small fire pit.

There was something comical about Candice's socks and hiking boots on her otherwise naked body. Patrick's black-and-white, high-top sneakers looked no less silly. They lathered each other up with Off. The mosquitoes had found them as soon as they had stopped moving. They sat on their ensolite pads in a spot where the sun broke through and had lunch. This was all fine, Patrick thought, but what do we do here for the next several days? He hadn't thought to bring anything to read.

Candice had a plan for that. She had been surprised when Patrick told her that he had never taken LSD. She thought everyone in their generation had been on acid trips, at least in San Francisco. She was still in high school when she started tripping. Patrick reminded her that he was a New Yorker, and all his trips had been on subways. Well, it was time for him to catch up and tune in.

"I don't like the phrase *drop out,*" Candice said. "Maybe *shift sideways* or *take off.*" Candice worked in PR. She was a good salesperson. "Your first trip and all, I'll be your guide. You can trust me totally. You must trust me totally. If things start getting weird for you—though it shouldn't; this is very good acid—I've brought a few joints that you can smoke and bring you in to a high you're more familiar with."

"Will you take some, too?"

"I wouldn't be a very good guide if I set you out on your

own. It's a different country. Think of it that way—that you're visiting a different country, where they speak a different language, have different customs."

"I've never been to another country besides Canada."

"Then don't think of it that way. Think of it any way you want to. Don't think at all. But it's not a fantasy. It's as real as this," Candice gestured around them, "more real."

It is truly pointless to try to describe an acid trip, either in words or images. The experience does not translate, and all attempts to do so—as Patrick remembered from his days at the *Oracle*—were as boring as listening to someone else's dreams. The experience itself was exhausting. Patrick slept well that night. And in the morning he had a strange hunger that he could not satisfy. He craved something like cheese, which Candice had not packed. She laughed at his voraciousness. But, on the second day, he was ready for, eager for, another dose of alternate reality. It felt like there was a lot to learn, and his trepidations had been silenced. This time he did not need a keeper. This time, after taking the acid, he headed off alone into the forest. It was beckoning him. He took off up their little stream, away from everything human, leaving Candice female tripping at the camp, weaving something out of plants she had gathered.

In addition to his sneakers and another coat of bug repellent, Patrick was wearing his belt today, with a holster attached that held Candice's collapsible hatchet. In retrospect that didn't make too much sense, but they had exhausted the supply of kindling and firewood around the camp, and Patrick thought he would bring some back.

He got lost in the wilderness. Where he belonged. But he never lost the sight or sound of their stream, his companion, his passage back. It was a wonderful day. Details could not delineate it. The whole was unexplainable. It wasn't meant to be explained. It was like a secret. He, Patrick, disappeared, absorbed into the luminosity surrounding him.

His rumbling empty stomach brought him back. The canyon was filling with shadows. He headed back downstream. As he got close to camp, he remembered the hatchet on his hip and why he had brought it. He remembered the woman Candice waiting at camp for firewood to cook his dinner. He remembered her attractiveness. He unholstered the hatchet and clicked its folding handle into place. He would bring her gifts of perfect firewood. He headed up the ridgeline above camp. He was an Indian now, a forest creature. He walked without making a sound. The hatchet in his hand was a tomahawk.

Something large moved in the boulder shadows of the stream below him. Was it a deer or a wolf? He froze and focused. He shifted and tightened his grip on the tomahawk. It moved again, upstream toward the camp. Patrick moved silently toward a spot on the ridge above it. It was a man, the bare back and buttocks of a man with long black hair crouched down behind a boulder. He was watching, stalking naked Candice as she moved about the campsite.

Patrick knew he could slaughter the stalker. He would land on him like a puma and his tomahawk would dispatch him with a few sure blood-spurting blows. Nothing had ever seemed so certain, so right. His muscles coiled for the spring, the proper moment. The war hoop gathered in his throat. Then a Patrick thought occurred to him—What would he do with the body? The stream would run red with his blood down to his tribe below. He paused, considering, still intent on the kill. Then Candice stopped and looked in their direction, as if she knew something was about to happen, and the long-haired naked man, as tan as an Indian, turned and snuck on all fours through the shadows downstream away from them.

The place Deborah found for Patrick was up Green Street, a couple of blocks above Columbus and only four blocks from Specs. She called it a penthouse, but it was just a few rooms on the top of a three-story apartment house. There were plenty of windows, and, it being near the crest of the hill, plentiful views, mainly of its neighbors. There was plenty of sunlight, but next to no furniture. Patrick took to it immediately. Its sparseness suited his mood. He had a queen-sized bed delivered and moved in the first of the month. Deborah helped him move. She brought one of her kids to help. There wasn't that much to move, but there were a lot of stairs. One of his new neighbors came up to make sure he didn't have a dog.

Patrick had to get a new phone number, as this neighborhood had a different exchange. He debated whether he needed a phone at all, as no one called; but mother Deborah wouldn't hear of it. "What about an emergency? Or if you want to order a pizza?" When it was installed, there were only three people he could think of to call and give the new number to—Douglas, Candice, and Joanna. Actually, he called Joanna just to see how she was doing, and when he mentioned he had moved she asked for the number. Joanna asked if he had seen Meredith. She called her Daisy. Joanna knew she had moved to the city, but that was all. Patrick decided not to mention the $400 meeting. But that made him think of Meredith, and after several calls he finally reached her.

"Uncle Rick? What's up?"

"Just checking in on my favorite niece."

"I thought I was your only niece."

"That too. Wanted to let you know I've moved, got a new number."

"Where to?"

"North Beach."

"Cool. Been to any more ball games? You still owe me a rain-check dinner."

He had to wait for her to find a pen to write down his number. She asked for his new address as well. "Maybe you could feed me in North Beach some night," she said.

Douglas had a theory about law enforcement. It all had to do with property, with protecting property. "The early, feudal stuff is pretty obvious—the people with property made all the rules. The church made up more rules to get their own property. The Constitution was written by dudes who owned property, including human property. You couldn't vote if you didn't own property. Property was power. Property gave you rights. Disrespect for property became immoral. You know, when white American Christians invaded the Pacific Northwest, the first new law they came up with was to make the native potlatch custom illegal. They were shocked, shocked, scandalized by the idea that a chief would hold a big party and give away all his wealth just for the hell of it. It was a sin. It went against the Bible.

"Of course, all this wasn't popular with the folks who didn't own property but wanted some, so the property owners had to hire enforcers. All well and good, the natural order. No one blames predators for liking to eat meat. Go somewhere else and get your own property. Leave mine alone. The problem arises with creating this enforcer class. Now that they have the borrowed power of the property owners behind them, they can start expanding their own power by making up their own laws. The propertied class is okay with that as long as the new laws seem to curtail the rights of the unpropertied. But other factors got involved, like religious beliefs and bigotry and twisted agendas and just plain human meanness. What the fuck does my going seventeen miles over the speed limit on an empty road in the middle of the night have to do with property rights? Who am I hurting by snorting cocaine?"

All Patrick could think of was that he didn't own anything, not even a car, much less real property. He had never voted. The only right he cherished was that of being left alone. He had neither use nor fondness for cops. Only once had he called them. It was when he was in night school at CCNY and living on the Lower East Side, in a one-room studio on East 3rd Street. One after-midnight, walking home from the subway, he saw two hefty white guys stealing motorcycles, big choppers chained to parking meters. They were lifting the bikes far enough off the ground to slip their chains over the top of the meters and putting them in the back of a rental step van.

Patrick watched them do it twice and got the truck's plate number as they pulled away. He didn't have a phone at the time, too poor, but he found a working pay phone and called the police to report what he'd seen, giving descriptions and the plate number along with his name and address. About twenty minutes later, back in his apartment, the outside buzzer buzzed—the cops. He let them in and waited at the door to his apartment. There were two of them. The first one slammed Patrick against the door with his forearm and held him there while the second slipped by them and went into his room. While cop #1 interrogated him, cop #2 ransacked the room. Patrick was waiting for the handcuffs, but they left as quickly as they had arrived, with one last slam into the door. That was the last he heard of it. It was also the last time he called the cops.

Douglas was riffing on law enforcement because he had to go to court. His lawyer had managed to massage away with fines the speeding ticket, the expired license, and the unpaid curb rent. He had the possession charge tossed on insufficient evidence—not enough cocaine left in the bindle. But the DUI charge remained.

"The next thing you know, we've got this industry—Law & Order, Inc.—employing millions of people, not just cops and courts, but lawyers and bail bondmen, prisons and weapons manufacturers, corporations and lobbyists and unions. One of our subsidiaries operates penitentiaries in five states. Did you know that? Another supplies security services for U.S. naval bases."

They were in Douglas's Pernod lounge.

"Fastest growing industry in the country. Like any commercial enterprise, it's subject to supply and demand, gotta have new laws to feed the whole system, justify its existence and expansion. That's the real reason why the U.S. has more people behind bars and at a higher per capita rate than any other country in the history of the world. It's good business."

"Yeah, but what are you going to do about it?"

"Whatever my lawyer tells me to do. It's his game. And I'll have another drink."

In court, Douglas's corporate lawyer got the DUI charge dismissed as well on the technicality that standard CHP procedures had not been followed. Douglas had not been pulled over for erratic driving but for speeding; the arresting officer did not aver that Douglas had smelled of alcohol or that he had sounded or acted drunk; and no field sobriety test had been administered. So, there were no grounds for someone else—unidentified—subsequently subjecting him to a breathalyzer test after he was in custody on a different charge. The judge bought it. He hadn't gone to as elite a law school as Douglas's lawyer.

That July, America's first planetary space probe, Viking 1, landed on Mars. The event meant absolutely nothing to Patrick. He couldn't see why it would mean anything to anybody. Rockets maybe. Fourth of July fireworks were patriotic. The rockets' red glare was in the national anthem. It was a weird guy thing. They had all these rockets but no current enemies they were allowed to fire them at, so shoot the moon, shoot a planet. Invent some bogus reason why it's a good idea. A neat, pointless job, pays well.

Joanna had a different hit on it. When she called and asked Patrick to stop up when he got the chance, she didn't say why. He brought barbeque. It took her a while to get around to the favor she wanted. She had a new work, a broadside she called it, that nobody wanted to publish. It wasn't a book or even a pamphlet. It was a long poem that she wanted to stand alone called "Sky Fucker." She wanted Patrick's help.

"I'm not a publisher, Joanna."

"You print things. Isn't that what publishers do?"

"I brush my teeth. That doesn't make me a dentist."

"No, you'll help me out. You know how these things work. It's your skill, it's what you do. Are you just a prostitute who does it only for money? Can you do it once for love of literature, for me?"

The poem was long, three double-spaced pages, and the lines were longer than in her earlier work. Patrick asked for her to read it to him, but she refused. "Some poems are written to be performed, recited. Others are meant just for the page, to be read alone. This is one of those." She left him with the poem.

"Sky Fucker" was, tangentially, about the Martian probe—she played with that word. The poem was in the form of a mother addressing her daughter, giving her worldly advice that the daughter did not want to hear. It was about desertion and denial, about America and men, about rockets and rape, orbits and obituaries. There were junk-yard dogs and flashes of pornography. The first time through, Patrick grasped mainly the anger. The second time through, not rushed by the poet's urgency, he could linger over the disparate, sometimes confounding images and try to intuit the point of the story that the mother was trying to tell.

Okay, it was a dismantling of American maleness, its boastful delusions and drastic ramifications. The most explicit rape was that of Gaia. That fit in with the scattered fragments about men deserting the mothers of their children. She only had to hint at rockets as penises, "fueled by menstrual blood." The rockets to outer space and other planets were only the male ego in denial, thinking it could abandon what it had defiled as it sought new targets to deflower.

"Then why Mars, not Venus?" the daughter asks.

"Homospatiality," the mother answers, "self-love."

Patrick was not a literary critic. The poem made him uneasy; it put hooks in him. When Joanna returned, he said, "But what do we do with it?"

Patrick took the poem to Rex, who loved it and showed it to Marna, who thought it "kicked ass." Patrick shared with them Joanna's desires for its printing.

"Leave it to me," Rex said. He designed it as a four-color poster. Patrick paid to have a hundred printed. Joanna approved of the final product, though she had no use for the color black.

Chapter 11

It was a beaut. Once he got her in the light where he could get a proper look at it. "That's going to be a gorgeous shiner. Can you see alright?"

Meredith closed her other eye. "A bit blurry."

Patrick wrapped some ice cubes in a towel and handed it to her.

"Does this help?"

"Don't know. It's what they do in movies." He brought her two aspirin. "Only pain pills I got. Want to tell me what happened?"

Meredith looked at the pills in his hand and shook her head. "I took something."

Meredith had been sitting on the front steps of his building when Patrick got home from his evening walk and a couple of drinks at Specs. She was holding her woven Mexican shoulder bag. When they got up to his place she went right to the loo. He didn't get a good look at her face until she came out.

"We had a fight. He won."

"Who he?"

"Eric, the man I've been living with."

"Any other injuries?"

"Bruises. This." She held out her half-clenched right hand, which was swollen with dried blood on the knuckles.

"And this." She lifted up her shirt, showing her belly and rib cage and the bottom of one breast. "I hope the rib is just bruised, not broken." There was a large red mark. "He hit me with a chair."

Patrick's instinct was to reach out and touch the spot. He stopped himself. "Want to go to the hospital, get it x-rayed?"

"What for? If it is cracked, they can't do anything for it."

Rage really was like a pot coming to boil. "Did you call the police?"

"No, but I told him I was going to. Can I stay here to-night, Uncle Rick? I have nowhere else to go."

"Of course. Can I get you anything? Have you eaten?"

"No, nothing. But could I have a drink? The pill I took works faster with alcohol."

All Patrick had in the house was an unfinished bottle of Stoli, nothing to mix it with. She drank it straight, still holding the ice pack to her face. She had trouble holding the glass in her damaged hand. She was just a kid being brave. It only took a few minutes for the pill, the vodka, and the shock, he guessed, to take effect. She put her head down on her folded arm on the table and passed out. Patrick hoisted her to her feet and helped her to the front room where a day bed served as a couch. He covered her with his only blanket, the same one her mother had slept under. He brought her Mexican net bag from the kitchen and put it on the floor be-side her. It was stuffed. For a while he stayed and watched her, watched her breathe. He was enraged at this Eric.

Patrick didn't know what angel dust was. "PCP," Meredith said, "a head tripper." In the morning, she was hungry. He fixed her what he always had for breakfast—instant oatmeal and toast, coffee. He called Rex at the office to say he wouldn't be in.

"Eric was a cokehead when we got together. That was alright, though he was getting sort of paranoid. But when he got into the angel dust, he started getting weird—pushy, possessive. I wanted to move out, but I had nowhere to go until the dorm opened up again. Then when he found out I'd had drinks with your pal Douglas, he had a fit. I was packing when he attacked me."

"Douglas?"

"Yeah. He's a strange dude, isn't he? Funny though."

Meredith spent the day in bed, recuperating. Patrick could tell by the way she moved that she was in pain, but she didn't complain. She had her pills. She slept and she watched TV. He went grocery shopping.

By the third day, the left side of Meredith's face was entering the purple/green phase, but she said her ribs were feeling better, so they probably weren't cracked. Patrick had returned to work, leaving her alone to convalesce. She liked the sun-filled rooms. "It's a relief not just being on my guard all the time. I don't know what I saw in him. The sex was really good at first."

"Write it off to hormones. We all make that mistake."

"But he was such a shit."

"Speaking of the shit, I'd like to find him and beat it out of him."

"He's gone, left town. I called a mutual friend, who said Eric split after I told him I was going to the cops. Now his paranoia has something real to gnaw on. He's from L.A., he probably went back there."

"Meredith, how about we let your mother know you're here?"

"Trying to get rid of me?"

"No, you're being here's no problem."

"How's mom doing?"

"Okay. She's got a new work out." Under Patrick's bed was a packet of "Sky Fucker" posters. He went and fetched one. Meredith was propped up in bed, a position her ribs requested. She held the poster at arm's length. Her face took on a faraway look. She tilted her head to one side and her eyes began to glisten with tears. She set the poster down on the bed and waved Patrick away.

"Going to the store. Want anything?" he said.

She just shook her head and waved him away.

"You know that four hundred dollars?" Meredith asked. They were seated at the kitchen table, eating ice cream. "Sky Fucker" was spread out on the table. She had dried her tears, but her one good eye was still puffy. "It was for an abortion. Mom knew about it and didn't approve. She thought I should have the baby, then give it to her to raise. I thought that was an awful idea, especially for the kid's sake. What if it was a boy? Could you imagine her raising a boy?"

"Was Eric the father?"

"Let's not go there. That's why we haven't talked since. That's what this part is about." She pointed to a few lines of the poem with the image of *rapists' offspring hanging from the trees*. "Uncle Rick, can I keep this?"

"Certainly. I've got more."

"Did you do this for her?"

"I had it done."

"I don't want her to see me looking like this. The explanations. It would only hurt her."

"It was just a suggestion."

"I have my own suggestion. Could we have Chinese take-out tonight? You still can't cook."

People of the woods. That's how Patrick saw them—a man, a woman, and three children. No four, the oldest daughter, a teenager, lagging behind on the trail. They were all, except for the youngest a boy of maybe five, carrying black plastic garbage bags. They emerged from the conifers on the trail in front of him. Patrick was headed up the trail. They were headed down. He was struck by how cheerful they seemed, and how foreign—teak-complexioned, their clothing not American. The father and mother smiled and nodded a greeting. "*Alo,*" the small boy said. He was grinning and holding a very large mushroom.

"Hello," Patrick said. They slowed as they approached each other. The trail was narrow. Patrick stepped off to let them pass. The boy stopped in front of him and proudly held up the mushroom for Patrick to admire. He said something in a language Patrick did not understand, which would have been any language besides English. Patrick smiled and nodded. The boy's eyes were a startling blue.

"He wants you to have it," the father said, in an accent Patrick had never heard before.

"Such a beautiful mushroom. No, I couldn't."

"No, take it. Make him happy. We have many." He held up his half-full garbage bag.

Patrick bent down and took the offered mushroom. The boy surprised Patrick with a kiss on his cheek. The mother laughed. They moved on down the trail. The teenage daughter paused as she passed, giving Patrick an appraising look. Holding his gaze and raising her eyebrows once, she conveyed a signal as old as the forest.

It was an encounter he would never forget. Especially as he was high on psilocybin at the time, his magic mushrooms, and the episode was resonant with hidden messages from his Fungod.

When Candice left—promoted to her D.C. office—she gave Patrick part of her stash of psilocybin. It came in recycled black-and-gray plastic Kodak 35-mm film canisters. Its provenance was a hippie ganja and shrooms plantation up in Alpine County. The mushrooms had been sun-dried and reduced to a powder the color and consistency of ashes. Each canister contained the psychedelic equivalent of maybe a half-dozen LSD trips, but voyages milder, more peaceful and natural than man-made acid. He also could control his dosage—one, two, or three lines of mushroom dust licked discretely from the palm of his hand.

The Fungod preferred that their sojourns together take place outdoors and solitary. There were too many people in San Francisco for solitude, but just across the Golden Gate in Marin were the forests of Muir Woods and Mt. Tamalpais, where, on the upper back trails, he could pass a day hiking, escaped from his species. Amazing what appears in the absence of humans. The raptors. All the eyes of the forest upon you as you pass. It was on such a three-line-lick hike on the back side of Mt. Tam, on a Fungod tutorial, that his gypsy mushroom messengers appeared.

The thing about the insights and wisdom that arrived with the Fungod's mentorship was that they did not apply in the other, everyday, simple world. They were irrelevant there. Of course, Patrick had to spend five days a week in that other world. He learned to think of it as a board game where he made his moves and others made theirs. He was an observer, but also a player in the performance. Sometimes, when another player aced a scene, Patrick would applaud. Rex would take a bow. With the Fungod's perspective, the meaningless became vaudeville; you could laugh. Life was a game.

On foul weather nights in the city, Patrick might do a one-line lick and hit the deserted back streets of his neighborhood, ending up at Specs for a warming shot of schnapps and a green death back. He had discovered that the Fungod was a friend of Bacchus. On nights like that at Specs there would be just the regulars, agreeable human nature to observe, performing their improv for his entertainment. There was no need of the back-bar mirror for him to see himself among them. The Fungod would share observations.

Petronella was one of the regulars. She was slight and dark and effected an austere defensive shield. One such night, seated on the stool beside Patrick, she asked, "Is there nothing you take seriously?" It wasn't an accusation. She meant it as a compliment. It started that simply. Beneath her tough-bitch disguise, Petra was just the skeptical girl next door. They shared a fondness for detachment, though she was more philosophical about it. She lived alone, a studio on Greenwich. He walked her home one night to get a book on Schopenhauer she wanted him to read (he never did). She didn't invite him up. He waited in the street. "The place is a mess," she said.

Petra liked to walk, and they took to taking late-night hikes together on evenings when Patrick was not with Fungod. She was a good trekking companion. She matched his pace and felt no need to talk. She admitted she felt safer on the streets with Patrick. She had her favorite vista destinations. "I like long views," she said. On one one-line-lick night, sitting at the bar, Petra suggested a hike, and Patrick declined, explaining that he only hiked alone when on mushrooms. This interested her, and she quizzed him. She had never tried psilocybin. LSD, of course. Peyote only made her nauseous. Marijuana always made her fall asleep. She asked to see it, and Patrick pulled the canister from his jacket pocket to show her. She asked if she could taste it and took a sample with a damp fingertip. The Fungod—on his second green death—said go ahead, and Patrick laid a line out on her palm and a line on his hand and showed her how to lick it off. They washed it down with ale.

Patrick was not opposed to routines. Board-game life was mainly composed of routines. Routines bestowed freedom. He had never held a repetitive, assembly-line-type job, but he imagined they could be very meditative. Muscle memory left your mind free to wander. Like playing solitaire. The same was true on a different scale about daily routines. Get up/piss/make coffee/shower/dress, and the next thing you know you're out of the house without even thinking about it. His ex-wife had been the queen of routines, probably still was. He couldn't see her changing. The ur-routine was having routines.

At work, the shop was running smoothly. Douglas left them alone. The crew was content. Rex kept things from falling through cracks. At home—he could think of his new place as home—his procedures and habits had assumed a familiar mindlessness that suited their lack of meaning. Meredith's week-long convalescence had interrupted his solo habitudes, but when she left to return to her dorm, the old mundane order swiftly returned. Living alone, he did not need to meld his routines with anyone else's, especially not with any arcane feminine demands of space and time. Stag existence suited him fine. He had zero desire to interrupt it.

As luck would have it, Petronella felt the same way about her life, but she liked getting laid now and then. Having an available occasional erotic partner freed both of them from other, potentially entangling relationships. They'd both been there. Petra's ex was in San Quentin. She had only distain for romance— "a sick attempt to give hormones subjective meaning." She didn't think much of meaning itself— "all invention." The search for meaning was only the insecure searching for self-definition by attributing meaning to externalities, "delusional." Was there any meaning to the phases of the moon or the movement of the stars? "No." Did a life have meaning? A death? "Impossible." According to Petra, all you could honestly know was where something fell on the spectrum between pleasing and unpleasing. Psilocybin was pleasing, so was coitus. Agreement was pleasing, but hardly necessary.

So, sometimes now their nighttime hikes would end up

at his place or hers, where they found pleasing release, but not meaning, in one another's bodies. It turned out the Fungod could also be the Fuckgod. Who knew?

Petronella also found alcohol pleasing. She credited AA with pushing her to nihilism. "When the bullshit gets too deep, you start looking for the bull and find the exit." Her ex had helped. "Orin taught me that the so-called truth was just someone else's loaded dice." She said she went to Specs to drink because she knew she would have to walk home, so she couldn't get hammered like she did if she drank alone at home. Not that she didn't drink at home. For such a small body, she had a surprising capacity for alcohol. Patrick never saw her stumbling, slurring drunk. In fact, the more she drank—slowly, sipping, savoring—the more precise and caustic she became. It was the fuel she burned.

Patrick stopped sharing his shrooms. He told Petra he was out, but actually he was afraid of exhausting his supply before discovering how to restock. And he had decided she did not need them—Ethanolia was her personal preceptor. Fungod returned to Patrick's private, occasional practice. As an unexpected ancillary result, he started drinking more when they were together. He was also drinking more on his nights out coking with Douglas. Dealing with hangovers became a new part of Patrick's routines.

Chapter 12

There was nothing hanging on Patrick's apartment walls, so he pinned up one of Joanna's posters in the kitchen. It was growing on him. Rex's design was nothing like the old *Oracle* psychedelic art. It was crisp, with solid colors and smooth lines. It pulled you in to read the words. He had another one simply framed and hung it in his office, where Douglas asked about it. He was surprised that the poem was by Meredith's mother. He hadn't known her mother was a poet. Funny, the things we don't know about one another, not so much the secret stuff, but everyday things, like families.

Everyone leaves their families behind. Relatives become history, a society of orphans. Patrick's only remaining family was his sister, and he hadn't even said goodbye to her when he left New York. Douglas had to have family back in Carolina, but he had never mentioned them. No one at the corporation would be so crudely sentimental as to have family photos on display in their office. Maybe it was for the best—unnecessary information, an impediment to rugged American individualism. He wondered how it was for rich kids, held by the lines of their family wealth.

When Patrick asked Petronella about her family, she became suspicious. She actually said, "What? Are you writing a book?" No, and he wasn't really interested in her family.

He was just curious what her reaction would be. In other places, other societies, your family was of paramount importance—all those Celtic O's and Mac's—but for most Americans it was a null set. Maybe because of all the divorces? Maybe because history in general meant nothing to them—all that shit had already happened. It was no part of them. The present and the immediate future were the only two tenses that mattered. Petra admitted she had changed her last name, Americanized it from the Flemish, because she didn't want anyone slapping an ethnic tag on her. "None of their business," she said.

Douglas was still pursuing Meredith. Late one afternoon he came into Patrick's office with three of Joanna's books he had picked up at City Lights. "Does she make any money on these?" he asked.

"She relies on food stamps," Patrick said.

"No wonder. They don't make much sense."

"They're not news releases. You got to bring something to them. Pretend you're a detective and the poems are notes left at the scene of a crime. Draw some conclusions."

"Should I mention to Meredith I bought them? If she asks me what I thought of them, what should I say?"

"Start with nothing. I doubt she has read them. Meredith is currently trying not to be her mom. And, if you're getting back into the tail-chasing game, why not go after someone closer to your own age who doesn't come with a reading list?"

Douglas plopped into a chair. "The ones my age have been in the game so long they're boring. How about Italian tonight? One of your places."

So, it was osso buco at Patrick's favorite counter place on

Broadway. Being in North Beach and only a few blocks away from Specs, Patrick took Douglas there for an after-dinner drink. Douglas hadn't been there before. He really wasn't impressed.

"My mother was into this trip—antiques, old stuff hanging on the walls. She was a Daughter of the Confederacy. The glorious past was still present in our parlor. My friends used to call our house the museum."

"Mom still alive?"

"Last I heard. She's been shunning me since my divorce."

"Father?"

Douglas gave Patrick a squinty look. "Yeah, I have one."

Petronella came in, and Patrick introduced them.

"I don't like Southerners," Petra said.

"Neither do I," Douglas answered. They got along fine.

"A concert? What kind of concert? I didn't know you went to concerts."

Douglas had called Patrick at home, which was weird.

"I don't, generally, but this is supposed to be a good one. Tickets are hard to get, and I've just been offered freebies, a bribe actually. I can get two more, if you want to come along."

"A double date? Will I have to buy a corsage?"

"Hardly, it's at Winterland Ballroom. Antibiotics might be more appropriate, that and some of your fancy fungi."

"Rock and roll," Patrick said.

"Before it vanishes or is outlawed."

"I never heard you listen to rock and roll."

"You never heard me listen to anything. You want to

come along or what? Bring Petronella. She'll dig it."

"When?"

"Thanksgiving. That seems properly inappropriate somehow."

"Who's playing?"

"The Band. It's being billed as their farewell appearance, their Last Waltz."

"You like The Band?"

"How can you dislike The Band?"

Joanna just showed up. Well, she had called a few days before to get his new address, but she arrived unannounced. Patrick was about to head out for dinner somewhere, he wasn't sure where—maybe just noodles at Wo's—when the street-door buzzer buzzed. Joanna was all dressed up—cowboy boots, a long denim skirt, a black turtleneck and green silk blouse, with an embroidered patch jacket of many colors, a leather shoulder bag. She looked good. She had a glow on. She was on her way to an event and wanted to pick up some of her poem posters.

As Patrick rolled up and wrapped in newspaper and tape some posters for her, Joanna asked if he had heard from Meredith recently. He hadn't.

"I was wondering how she is doing," she said. "I can't reach her. I leave messages; she doesn't call back. Her father died. I wonder how she's taking it."

"Oh."

"OD'd, drugs-and-booze-suicide roulette."

"Sorry."

"Don't be. He was a shit, and he knew it. Self-disgust

killed him."

"I'll give her a call."

"Let me know, no matter what her news is." Joanna took the roll of posters and left.

Lo mein at Wo's. Patrick didn't go to Specs after. Instead, he hiked to a lookout point in the Presidio where he could see the bay and the lights of the Golden Gate. He hadn't thought of his dad's death in years, the night the ambulance did not come, and he sat there alone, listening to the death rattle fade in the old man's chest.

Douglas hadn't spoken with Meredith in weeks. He had pretty much given up the chase. "Too fine for the likes of me." But he did have her new dorm phone number. Whenever Patrick dialed it, it just rang. He managed to reach the dorm office and left a message.

The truth, as opposed to fact, is an agreement. If two people see a tree fall into a lake, they can agree that it happened. If only one person sees a tree fall into a lake and tells a second person about it, the second person, to make it true, must agree by accepting the account. But if person number one says the falling tree struck the skiff in which his wife was leaving him, killing her, person number two, to make it true must—not having witnessed the event—agree, trusting the teller's veracity. Seeing as it is just an agreement, the truth does not necessarily have to reflect anything actual.

Patrick was not naturally skeptical. Being suspicious can take a lot of energy. He was a face-value guy. He wouldn't know—wouldn't really care—if the rolled-up twenty he used to vacuum a line of cocaine was counterfeit. The fact is that truth, the whole truth, and nothing but the truth had little utility in the day-to-day. So be it and so what? Fibs greased the wheels of social interaction. If a statement purported to be factual was egregiously unacceptable as true, it needed to be called out as such. But did it really matter, say, if someone's excuse for being late was obviously bogus? It only matters in your evaluation of how much to trust that person in future requests for agreement. Liars lose your trust.

Petronella had a strange relationship with the truth. Patrick noticed it first in her inconsistencies. She didn't seem to mind contradicting herself. He didn't bother calling her on it. He would get the feeling as she was relating things that had happened to her that she was constructing them as she reported. None of it was essential. It was just chit-chat. Then one night she said something that was so contrafactual that Patrick felt impelled to correct her. Jimmy Carter had been elected President a few days before, and Petra made a pronouncement about Southern men that was just silly. He had never tried to correct her before.

She was unfazed. She made up another non-fact to support the first. They were walking at the time, just the two of them, on Filbert Street.

"Is this a test?" Patrick asked.

"What kind of test?"

"A reality test. Do you expect me to agree with you?"

"No reason for you to agree with me. Don't bother yourself."

"That doesn't bother you? That I can't agree with you?"

"Why should it bother me? Does it bother you that I may not agree with things you think?"

"But there is reality, objective fact."

"All facts are just ideas. You'd like to make me think like you think. Mental rape. I don't have to think like you. I can have my own thoughts."

Patrick dropped it. This was beyond his scope of responsibility.

A block or so later, Petra continued, "Your truth is just a masculine conspiracy, a cliché version of what's really going on, which you expect the rest of us to swallow. True reality is freedom from truthism, allowing for all possibilities."

He never questioned her again. The link between them was tenuous enough.

Meredith called that Sunday, early. Well, not that early. Patrick was almost awake but only vaguely alive. It had been a late Saturday night with Douglas. He asked if he could call her right back. He had to take a leak and fix some coffee.

"Mother have you check up on me?" Was Meredith's first question.

"What's family for?"

"I'm glad you answered the phone and not your girlfriend," she said.

"Which girlfriend would that be?"

"I never got her name. How many women live with you?"

"Why, none."

"Come on, Uncle Rick. I met her, or rather was attacked by her."

"What? When? What are you talking about?"

"Yesterday morning when I stopped by your place. Don't tell me she didn't tell you about her heroic defense of your virtue?"

Yesterday morning. He had woken up in his bed with Petronella. Interesting, how little space she took up. Friday night had been their party night. His hangover craved coffee and a diner breakfast. Petra was still sounders. Having her there always made him uneasy; she didn't fit somehow. She didn't like being there either, except for the sex. Last night they'd taken Quaaludes. He got dressed and left. Took his time getting back. Petra was gone when he returned.

"I guess she thought I was one of your squeezes, because she put on a doozie boundary/possession display. Women are so weird sometimes. She called you her man and your place her home. So, I figured she was living there with you. You poor guy. Is she often like that? She wouldn't listen to a word I had to say. She even threatened me. When she started going through the kitchen drawers, looking for a knife, I left."

Patrick could think of nothing to say, he was too angry, with both Petronella and himself. Alternate realities—dandy mental games, but dangerous if they escape into the actual world. Why had he allowed himself to get sucked into hers? He managed a brief apology to Meredith. That he wasn't that woman's man, that it wasn't her home, she did not live there, that she was only an occasional sexual partner.

"Maybe you should explain that to her," Meredith said.

"I didn't think she was that crazy. Sorry."

"Sorry for what? It's none of my business. I should have called first."

"What should I tell your mother?"

"Tell her I'm fine, that I'll be up to see her soon. I have

some things dad left for me to give her. And, Uncle Rick, get rid of that bitch."

When Patrick asked Petronella if anyone had stopped at his place Saturday when he was out having breakfast, she attacked him for not waking her and taking her along. When he pressed her, she said someone had come to the door as she was leaving, a saleswoman selling something. Petra had told her that he wasn't home.

After Petronella found out about the tickets, there was no way she wasn't going to the Band concert. Patrick hadn't told her; Douglas had brought it up one night at Specs. Patrick hadn't mentioned it to her because he wasn't sure if he wanted to go himself. All those people, all that noise, and going with Petra made it sort of a date. They didn't date. Not Patrick, Douglas, nor Petronella had family to spend Thanksgiving with, but it never occurred to them to have dinner together. Douglas said meet him at his Pernod bar, and they would go together in a taxi cab. The Winterland Ballroom—it had once been an ice-skating rink—was out on Sutter.

Petronella got it into her head that she needed to experience this historic occasion on psilocybin. Patrick didn't think so. This was not a Fungod event. *No* was not in Petra's functioning truth set. She knew he was holding out on her. She got a bit nasty. But by Thanksgiving night when she arrived at the bar, she had calmed down. She was smiling and cordial. She had a few Pernods with Douglas. Patrick could tell she was high on something. Douglas was by himself. He said he was going to meet someone there and excused himself to get up and make a phone call to check. Standing behind Petra, Douglas gestured to Patrick, then touched his nose and pointed to the gents, nodding in that direction. Patrick squinted and gave a minimal shake of his head. While Douglas was gone from the table, Patrick asked Petra what she was on.

"Well, you wouldn't share your mushrooms. I got something even better, some Angel Dust."

The scene outside Winterland was as packed and chaotic as Patrick had feared. There were policemen and police barricades. They joined the end of a line. Patrick was glad he wasn't on any drugs. Douglas left them in line and went off to hunt for his guest. The crowd was making Petra antsy. She was shooting looks at people. She lit a cigarette. A woman behind them in line coughed dramatically and said, "Please."

Petra turned and thrust her pack of Winstons at her. "Want one?"

The woman took a step backwards. "No."

"Then shut the fuck up."

The bearded guy beside the woman looked at Patrick and said, "Hey."

The line began to creep forward toward the corner of the building, where it turned to the front entrance. Douglas was standing there, waiting for them. Standing beside him was

Meredith. They ducked into line in front of them. The guy behind them said "Hey" again.

Petra said, "Stuff it." She was focused on Meredith. "So, you two pass your pieces of ass around, huh?"

Meredith was a good six inches taller than Petronella. She gave her a quizzical look.

"Or is she just a convenient whore?" Petra added. The line was still moving forward, but Petra wasn't budging. Douglas and Meredith were staring at her.

Recognition registered on Meredith's face. "Oh, it's you. Uncle Rick, didn't I recommend that you ditch this bitch?"

It was like an explosion. Petra sprang at Meredith, grabbing a handful of hair and a handful of jacket. Meredith fought her off with a punch to her side. Within seconds it was a melee. Patrick tried to restrain Petra. Douglas was trying to separate them. The bearded man and his mate joined in. Punches were thrown. Others tried to interfere. A woman went down. Panic spread through the closely packed crowd. The cops arrived with their nightsticks.

At the precinct, it was determined that no one was hurt beyond bruises and scratches. The four of them were booked for public peace disturbance and spent the night in separate cells.

The Friday after Thanksgiving is generally observed as a holiday, but Douglas got through to the corporate lawyer. Patrick and Meredith were released with future court dates. Douglas and Petronella were not so fortunate. Douglas had been packing more cocaine for the concert, and Petra had so much PCP on her that she was booked on suspicion of being a dealer. Meredith joked that she could brag about her night in jail to her mother, who had a long history of Public Peace busts.

On Monday, Patrick was back at work, but Douglas was still in jail. In fact, Douglas never came back to work. Through Rex, Patrick learned that Douglas was officially on leave while his case was pending.

"He ain't coming back," Marna said. "You only get to use their lawyer twice. It's two strikes and you're out here."

Two weeks later, Patrick learned that he also was out of a job. A "reorganization" under a new VP. "Collateral damage," Marna said. He had two months to find a new position or it was unemployment. It had been a decade since his last time on the dole. He knew he couldn't do it now, not here. It was time to move again.

2006

Chapter 13

There was nothing charming about the place. Well, they had once gone to the trouble of painting the cement block walls. Blacktop landscaping. There was a warehouse on one side and a paint store on the other. All the ambience a jail deserved. Heartland Villa Nursing Home, the sign said, death row for the unconvicted. The neighborhood was appropriate. The inmates didn't care what was outside. The aperture of aesthetics, along with everything else, shrinks with age. Three squares and a cot, a walker maybe, a TV set. Outside was like the past, there but already gone. There was no escape. All the exit doors were locked.

It was hot in dismal Novato. Patrick sat in his air-conditioned rental car in the parking lot. He had forgotten how depressing America could be, even California. He didn't have to go in. According to Meredith, Joanna wouldn't care if he was there or not, wouldn't remember. She had no power of memory. An ambulance backed up to a side door. When he was a kid in New York they had been called meat wagons. A pick-up or a delivery? From where he was parked he couldn't tell. Not knowing what else to bring, he had brought flowers. Now, they struck him as funereal. In Hong Kong, cemeteries were vertical walls built on cliffs, with rows and rows of safe-deposit-box-sized stone repositories where you could stash the honorable deceased's ashes for as long as you wished to lease the space. Rent a tomb—Patrick's kind of realism.

Patrick's culture shock on his return to the States was more pronounced than it had been when he departed for elsewhere. America was a land of many strange poses and attitudes—and so many white people, so many grossly overweight. When you live in a place where your race is an almost invisible minority, you become hyperaware of your fellow expats. They represent you in a certain way. We all look alike to the natives, for one thing, and your compatriots' boorish behavior, even their dress, reflects on you. By and large, Americans were embarrassing. It was a discomfiting country of origin.

Well, he had come all this way What else would he do with the flowers? What had he been thinking? The idea had seemed sweet, fitting, almost romantic. Now it seemed stupid, sentimental, pointless. It was like taking flowers to a gravesite, only Joanna was not yet dead. He wasn't doing this for her. He was doing this for himself, faking a virtue, so that he could report to Meredith he'd done it. He had no use for the past. Why was he going there? It had been thirty years since he'd seen Joanna.

From his rooms in Cheung Chau he could see an old junk anchored in the rock-bound cove. It leaked oil, not black petroleum oil but something translucent that left a shimmering snake's tail on the outbound and inbound tides. It was a fixture there, one of the reasons he had taken the rooms, like a vessel abandoned from another era. Then one day it was gone, and nothing replaced it. The rooms were available because the house was jinxed. Locals wouldn't live there. A lane ended across the road from the house's never-opened front door, and superstition dictated that this left the place vulnerable to bad spirits coming down the lane. There must have been anecdotal evidence.

It was a big house. Patrick shared it with four or five other male Caucasians immune to Mandarin occultism. They were all journalists, mostly Brits, who, like Patrick, couldn't afford the rents in Hong Kong or Kowloon. Cheung Chau was affordable because it was the outermost island in the territory, the longest ferry ride from Victoria. Few other whites lived on the crowded rock. There were no motor vehicles on Cheung Chau. The narrow preindustrial lanes and cart tracks disallowed them. The lack of silence there was not mechanical. It had its own aroma. It was on the edge of the South China Sea. It smelled of kitchens and fishing boats, people and incense, the musk of old houses.

The ferry ride from Victoria could take an hour, more if it was foggy. One night in dense fog, the ferry pulled into the wrong harbor for safety, one island over, which was outside the territory, inside mainland China's waters, and the boat, with all its crew and passengers, was seized and held for days. In '76, when Patrick arrived, the border was strictly enforced. But the ferry ride was one of the plusses. His commutes were the pleasurable bookends of his work day. In the morning, coffee and buns and the *South China Morning Post* in the upper-deck first-class lounge, and in the evening—always on the last departure—cocktails and camaraderie in the same lounge. The camaraderie was with his housemates and other journalists returning to their tiny white colony. There was a bar at the dock in Cheung Chau and a few restaurants. It was usually late by the time he strolled home up the dark, quiet, deserted lanes, listening to other peoples' lives behind the shuttered windows.

Maybe returning had been a mistake. He had perfected that habit. San Francisco had been a default destination. When he left Kuala Lampur, Patrick didn't know where else to go. All forward progress had been halted years before. He could only go backwards. Asia was over. How had his new boss at his last job put it? Patrick's skill set had been eclipsed by new-age advancements. Not to mention that all of Southeast Asia had gone sour on Americans. They had never been liked, now they were no longer necessary. Only tourists would be tolerated. Time to retire.

When Patrick first arrived in Hong Kong, he was welcome. They were going through a Yank withdrawal. When the U.S. capitulated in Viet Nam in '75, it pretty much deserted the region, turning its back on the embarrassment. He quickly found an opening, managing production for a glossy visitors-bureau mag—the first of many gigs. He hadn't especially liked unknowable Hong Kong, but he had Cheung Chau and he discovered opium.

Joanna was asleep. A pleasant, fat woman in nurse's whites went to find a vase for Patrick's flowers. When she returned, she offered to wake Joanna, but Patrick said, no, let her sleep. He'd wait. It was cold in the room. Joanna was under a blanket. Her white hair was cropped close, like a prisoner's. He couldn't see her face, turned toward the wall.

There was a cork bulletin board, overfull with push-pinned stuff, not just papers and drawings but, well, stuff—sugar packets, a blue surgical glove, the torn-off front of a popcorn box, a Mamas and Papas LP cover, pieces of burned toast, a man's untied bow tie, and more. Beneath all this camouflage was a worse-for-wear copy of her Sky Fucker poster. The room was too cold, like a morgue. He left quietly, careful not to disturb her. At the street door he had to wait for someone to come and buzz him out.

It wasn't San Francisco. It was just another city. Hong Kong, Singapore, Kuala Lampur, Manhattan, San Francisco—they had all become the same, no matter what language the neon signs used. His generation had overseen this homogenization, this diminishment of otherness. Patrick missed the old city, the one that moved slower and paid more attention, the one wealth hadn't stifled. The one where you could still smoke in saloons.

Specs was still there, amazingly enough, still stuck, unchanged in its dead-end alley. Of course, everyone he had known was long gone. The new crowd was better dressed and less scruffy, but still not touristy—locals. The tourists would stand in the alley and look in, as if it really was a museum display. They still had green death and no lite beers for sale. In the old days, if someone asked for a lite beer, Specs would draw them a draft lager and, disdainfully, toss in two ice cubes. The bartenders were still from Dublin.

Patrick was staying at Meredith's. She had a big house on Twin Peaks that she shared with a woman named Chandra. Patrick had yet to meet Chandra. She was in Paris or London or someplace, doing whatever it was she did. Meredith wasn't around that much ether. She was a busy woman. Her job was down in Palo Alto, at Stanford, where she was an acquisitions editor at the University Press, but that seemed almost a sideline to her other activities. Patrick wasn't interested. He tried to stay out of her way and out of her life, which wasn't hard. It was a big house. It was also complete. The house was equipped with the full panoply of domestic appliances and amenities, everything from security cameras to a jacuzzi, an unused chef's kitchen and an almost empty wine cellar. It was furnished and decorated like one of those mansions in the Asian edition of *House & Garden* he'd worked for in Singapore. He could see the multipage layout. There were more bathrooms than he knew of. It was like a movie set, only nothing was being filmed there. Meredith and Chandra and gotten it all, down to bidets and a cleaning crew. The cleaning crew did not speak English.

It was also an indictment. Their perfect house was testimony to their success, to their talents and energies well spent. What did Patrick have to show for his forty years of work? The contents of his two pieces of luggage and briefcase. No more than he had started out with. Uncle Rick, the ne'er-do-well.

For a ne'er-do-well, he took a lot of taxis. Twin Peaks was beyond hiking distance. The closest neighborhood with bars and restaurants was downhill in the Castro at the outer end of Market Street. The Castro District had evolved from gay rebellious to gay swank. Homosexuality was now fashionable. One evening in a bistro there, Patrick saw someone he thought was Rex. Then he realized that if it was Rex, he had barely aged in thirty years. It was a next-generation Rex clone. But it made Patrick wonder if Rex was still around. Patrick had a problem the old Rex could solve. He had always been a ready source of street drugs. Maybe he could find some opium for Patrick. He needed some. He craved its familiar safety and escape. Booze didn't do it.

Patrick had gone through his withdrawals in Honolulu. He had stopped there for that purpose. He knew what to expect when he had to leave his opium behind in Kuala Lampur. He had gone through it before, every time he had moved and had to find a new supplier. It was like an intense, nervous flu. Four days of aches and sweats and nausea, runny nose and eyes and sleeplessness, diarrhea, cramps and an unshakeable sense of doom. What better place to suffer through it solo than a banal room in a Waikiki tourist hotel?

He still had Rex's Bernal Heights address in an old address book, the one with all the X'd-out entries. The cabbie had no problem with going there. Patrick remembered the block. It had changed. The row of once neglected, rundown, cookie-cutter bungalows was now a colorful chorus line of real-estate pride. Rex's place, once the spiffiest, was now the most subdued and historic looking. Patrick had the cab wait. When he pushed the doorbell, the dog barked twice. Rex answered the door. Patrick waved the cab away.

"Where ya been?" Rex said and gave Patrick a hug. Before- and after-photos. Although in his mind Patrick's appearance had not much changed, he knew—mirror knowledge—he was gaunter and greying and balding. Rex's appearance had evolved with the times—silver hair pulled back in a ponytail, a white goatee, a diamond ear stud. Rex was retired. Raul was gone, dead in the AIDS epidemic. He had no idea what had happened to Douglas. When Patrick asked about finding some opium, Rex said it was hard to come by in San Francisco, but that other opioids like heroin and methadone and oxycodone were readily available.

"So, that's the reason you looked me up," Rex said, "to score some drugs? I'll give you a name and a number. I'll call ahead to clear you. But, Patrick, don't come back."

It was a long hike down to Mission Street. In his Asian cities sojourn, Patrick had lost his love of walking.

When Patrick was in third grade at the Holy Name of Jesus parish school on the Upper West Side, they were testing the first polio vaccine. Catholic kids made good guinea pigs. They had no choice. The nuns lined them all up and told them to roll up their right sleeves. And they were stuck with big needles. Three separate times. Half of them got the vaccine, half got a placebo. Months later they learned who got which. Patrick was in the placebo group that had to go through it all again. Patrick always said he was allergic to placebos. The lasting effect was his fear of needles. He even knew the medical term for it—"trypanophobia." So, he was happy with the black tar heroin he got from Lorenzo—if that was his actual name—not only because it was cheaper, cruder, and uncut, but he could smoke it instead of injecting it—"chase the dragon" as they said in Hong Kong—just like he had his opium.

Nothing had changed in the valley. Interstate 80 was still the same. Flat as Nebraska, except for those white-toothed Sierra peaks appearing on the far horizon. Tahoe bound, Meredith's car. She had dozed off in the passenger's seat after Sacramento. She had a meeting or a conference or something in South Lake Tahoe and had asked Patrick to come along. She said it was because she felt bad about spending so little time with him, but he suspected she wanted a chauffeur. He didn't mind. It wasn't like he had anything else to do, although driving was still strange. He hadn't driven during his thirty years in Asia. His mind kept drifting away. He was on cruise control. All he had to do was steer, and on this highway as straight as a laser, even that was barely necessary.

He was pondering something Meredith had said earlier, around Vacaville, that life was a game of solitaire—the only person who knew if you cheated to win was yourself. They had been talking about partners. He didn't see how that fit. He understood the solitary part. The CHP passed him doing at least a hundred. Patrick hadn't seen him coming. If you were the law, you could break the law. Was that cheating? What was winning? How did you know when you'd won? In life it certainly wasn't who finished first. Premature death, premature ejaculation. Another CHP whizzed past him. Emergency or end of shift? Shiftless, that's what he was now, shiftless.

"What are you laughing about?" Meredith asked. Her eyes were still closed.

"Did you ever learn how to drive a stick shift?"

"No, never owned one. Before my time."

"When I learned to drive it was called standard."

"A clutch means something different to my generation."

"A shiftless generation."

"That was worth laughing about?"

"No. Sorry to disturb your rest."

"I'm only a decade younger than you, Uncle Rick. Does that count as a generation?"

"History changes speed. The closer we get to the present, the faster things happen. You could say the Dark Ages were a generation that lasted a thousand years. Nothing changed. Nothing new was generated."

"I don't know, I wasn't there," Meredith said, "but your generation pretty much blew it, didn't it? I mean, the time was ripe for change, for a revolution. Some of you got it started, then didn't finish the job. Got stoned and wandered off into the suburbs. Or Asia."

"Middle age."

"An excuse."

"A good one. What's your generation's excuse?"

"Menopause."

They both laughed.

The traffic slowed for the accident, even though the road was clear. The troopers were parked on the shoulder; two cars were crunched together in the roadside ditch.

Here's another view of the future—just get rich. That will change everything, right? Today you're poor; tomorrow you're not. Simple. It was like the floor of a factory—rows and rows of machines, each with its diligent worker plugging away, trying to cross over to that tomorrow. All the lights could be distracting, but they were not distracted. Some worked the slots and the poker machines with admirable speed and dexterity. Patrick had seen it all before, in Macau, but there the legions of hope addicts had all been slim Chinese. Here in Stateline, Nevada, they were all obese Americans.

Patrick didn't play. It was called play, but it was anything but a game. He sat at the bar and watched. Such a free pleasure, feeling superior. Inside his protective black-tar bubble, sipping his Moscow Mule, looking down on those poor slobs encaged by their ludicrous habit. Meredith was at her meeting. He had the day to himself and had strolled the few blocks from their resort hotel across the border to the first big casino on the Nevada side. Drinks were always cheaper in casinos. Their suite was on Meredith, as was the fancy meal they'd had the night before. She insisted the trip was her treat. It was all on one expense account or another. This was some sort of start-up venture she was involved with, another level of gambling altogether, also not a game, although sprung from the same aspiration—the pot of gold, the next level of wealth. The machines they played on were laptops.

Over dinner, Meredith told Patrick about Mark Twain's forest fire. A hundred and fifty years before, when Tahoe was still wilderness, Twain had come on a camping trip here, escaping Virginia City. An inept woodsman, his campfire got away from him and he started a fast-spreading forest fire. Trapped by the fire, his only way out was through it. Panicked, he went into the smoke only to discover that the fire was just a few feet wide, burning off what duff had gathered on the forest floor since the last fire had passed, and he ducked through unscathed.

She told it as if it was an obvious parable, but Patrick was unsure what lesson was to be drawn from it.

Chapter 14

You've got to celebrate the little things, especially if the little things are all there is to celebrate. For instance, there was no cat in Meredith and Chandra's house. Two American women and no cat? How rare was that? Patrick had no use for cats, a fact he had trouble hiding. Worthless creatures, as far as he could see—irritating, pointless, smelly house pests—and he was allergic to them. Cats were not allowed in Singapore housing. That made so much sense. He figured he had probably eaten cat in Hong Kong and Kuala Lampur. After thirty years living in places with neither pets nor lawns, America's addiction to both seemed absurd. There was a dog run—a big, empty, fenced-in patch of dirt, a wasted expanse of valuable real estate—in Eureka Valley that he passed on his way down to Castro Street. Gays loved their canines, the more outré the better. Patrick had read somewhere that America spends almost as much on its pets as it does on incarcerating all of its record number of prisoners. What a weird country.

When Patrick complimented Meredith on her freedom from felines, she gave him a squinched-up look. "I've never liked cats. You know that. You took me to the zoo once to scare me by showing me big ones."

"And Chandra?"

"Chandra doesn't have time for pets, doesn't need them."

"How will she feel about a house guest?"

"I don't know. It's never come up."

"I could be out of here in an hour."

"I doubt that will be necessary. We'll wait and see what Chandra says. Mom always said it was handy having a man around the house, as long as you didn't have to sleep with him."

"Whatever happened to the place in Bolinas?"

"I sold it when mom went into the nursing home. The house was useless, dangerous, falling down, but property values on the mesa had exploded. It's paying for her care."

"When do you expect Chandra back?"

"I never know. I'm not her keeper."

"I sell art," Chandra said, "lots of it, job lots of it. You know, the prints you see in hotel rooms. I run a service that puts them there." They were seated on the small balcony off the living room. The view was north, over rooftops, toward the cityscape, all the new skyscrapers almost hiding the old iconic pyramid. They were drinking chilled Chardonnay, just the two of them, Patrick and Chandra, in the middle of a weekday afternoon. "It's good to be back. I missed this place, this city."

She had surprised Patrick. He was fixing himself lunch when she came in the front door. He helped her bring her luggage up from the curb, then shared his lunch with her. The Chardonnay on the balcony was her idea. She had changed into shorts and a t-shirt. Meredith had forewarned her that her Uncle Rick was visiting. Chandra was older than Meredith, closer to Patrick's age. She was tall and slim, sharp featured. She had not bothered to hide her greying temples. She knew Patrick had been living in Asia and she was full of questions. She didn't ask when he was leaving.

It was the only game Patrick had learned how to play, but it had been thirty years. His first wife had been a backgammon player, and when they were courting he had had no choice. She liked winning. He had learned how to lose to pacify her. Chandra just liked to play. If she saw there was no chance of her winning, she would laugh and capitulate, start a new game. It was mainly just a chance to chat. They had plenty of opportunity. She had been on the road working for four weeks; now she was taking a break, working from home. Meredith was as busy as always.

If what you learn about a person comes only from them, you don't know what's being left out or what's being embroidered. Nothing wrong with that. You're not a detective investigating a crime. They are creating for you an intimate gift—the person they want you to know. You get to reciprocate. No one is the same person to everyone. The shifts in disguise may be minor or subtle, but they're real, they're intentional. Even the oldest of friends have their secrets. And, of course, we all lie to ourselves as well, mainly lies of omission. Denial is not just a river in Egypt.

Patrick and Chandra's chats over the backgammon board as they rolled their dice and made their moves, wandered, after a few days, from the banal into the slightly more personal. He learned that Chandra was not her given but her chosen name. She had grown up as a Nancy, Nancy Bennett. She became Chandra Porter-Benet when she launched her career. "I was no longer Nancy. I had always disliked being Nancy."

One afternoon, Chandra mentioned that when she was a young girl she had a fondness for hiding, for disappearing, so that her parents had to search for her, call out her name. It wasn't for fun; she was punishing them. Patrick said his son had the same irritating predilection at that age.

"Your son? I didn't know you had a son. Is there a wife as well? Ex- or otherwise? Meredith never mentioned an aunt and cousin."

"I *had* a son," Patrick said. He had become so relaxed around Chandra that he had accidentally broken a story barrier, opened a door he meant to keep locked. "Meredith doesn't know about them."

"Oh, I'm sorry. None of my business." Chandra was shaking the dice in her cup longer than usual. When she spilled them out, she said, "Did he die?"

"No, he didn't die. He's just no longer mine."

"Whose son is he then?"

"His mother's, her family's, his stepfather's, China's."

"You left him in China?"

"Yes. Make your move."

She made her move, and there was a long silence while he took his turn.

When Chandra got the dice back, she said, "You don't want to talk about it." Roll of dice. "But now I am intrigued. Was your wife Chinese? Why not talk about it?"

"The past is just luggage."

"Remember when people put stickers on their luggage, bragging where they had been?"

"No."

"Did you ever send postcards?"

"I was never a tourist."

"Was she pretty?"

"An Ornamental? No, nothing delicate. She was from the north, tall, big-boned and strong. And she wasn't my wife."

"What happened?"

"When the Brits gave up and left in '97 and the border was opened, she went back to her family on the mainland."

"With your son."

"With her son."

"Did he have a name?"

"She changed it."

"Do you miss him?"

"I was not a good father. I wish I had the chance to make up for that."

They were still playing, taking their turns. She was winning. "Was that because of your drug habit?" They stopped playing. Chandra reached out and put her hand on the back of his. "Patrick, I can smell it on you, smell it when I pass your room. It's an intriguing odor. Is it opium?"

"Something like that."

"Let's go out to dinner tonight. Meredith is stuck in Seattle and won't be home. Chinese?"

They said on the news that it was the worst heat wave in San Francisco's recorded history. People were dying, they said. But then people were always dying. Why blame the heat? It wasn't especially hot by Kuala Lampur standards, but one amenity the house did not have was central air-conditioning. This was Twin Peaks, up in the ocean breeze zone, where fog was your regular neighbor and you kept the heat on much of the year. The middle of summer, fog season, and there was no fog. Wildfires inland. Maybe there was something to all the global-warming panic. The city below was bathed in an out-of-focus haze like a fading memory in aspic. On TV they warned against taking your dog out for a walk, for the dog's sake. There seemed to be more sirens in the muffled distance. They went to the beach.

Not far, just down to Ocean Beach. Meredith wanted to stay in the air-conditioned car, but Chandra and Patrick made her come along. Other folks had had the same escape plan, but it's a big beach and people spread themselves out. It seemed the natural thing to do, to put maximum distance between you and strangers. This was not a communal event. They migrated south, toward the zoo. They took off their footwear and walked at the edge of the surf. Patrick had never seen Chandra and Meredith together before. Oh briefly, housemates in passing, but since Chandra's return Meredith had been especially busy. There was an imminent book-trade show in Frankfurt she had to attend, things to get done before she left. He dawdled behind them, feeling like someone who should be somewhere else.

They walked together, talking, several feet apart, carrying their sandals. They could be sisters. He had never seen them exhibit any intimacy, no public displays of affection. He thought he overheard his name mentioned and he fell even farther behind. Patrick had been raised to think women a mystery. "Don't waste your time trying to figure them out," his father had told him. Nuns were their most cabalistic manifestation, morals dominatrices, dressed like witches. He knew the now politically correct behavior was to treat women the same as you would a man, but that was impossible. With men you didn't have to be always on your guard. With men you were an equal, and they had to earn your respect; with women, respect was an obligation. Men were easy to ignore; women not so easy. Why had all his major social failures and fuck-ups involved a woman?

He knew he was a lousy lover. He'd been told. There were many unshared orgasms. But sex, the act, had little to do with it, with the basic reality. Women held the real power, men just the trappings. But their power was veiled in secrets. Meaning—if there was such a thing—lurked and migrated inside their mystery. Why else have artists always held the female form to be the paradigm of truth and beauty? He was old enough now, getting post-hormonal, to be philosophical about it. It wasn't just reproduction. The deeper the truth, the more complex the causes. He lacked understanding. He was not a deep thinker. He had known Meredith for forty years, and today she seemed brand new to him. He had known Chandra less than a week, and he sensed she knew his thoughts.

When Meredith left for Europe, Patrick was still at the house; so was Chandra. She would be going back on the road soon, though just in the region this time. She said that if Patrick wanted to stay on for a while, at least until Meredith returned, she wouldn't mind. She would appreciate having someone in the house when they both were gone. He had nowhere he was supposed to be.

But her first trip was to Oaxaca, and she asked Patrick to come along. "I've been there twice before, and the fact is the men there can be a real pain in the ass for an unaccompanied businesswoman. I'll just charge them for an assistant."

"A bodyguard?"

"In the literal sense. Hands off. The client is a resort hotel. They'll put us up. So it's just the flight expense. It'll let me pad my bill. Hell, I'll even pay you."

"A paid vacation?"

"But no sick leave, so be careful what you eat."

"What am I supposed to be assisting you with, aside from beating off wolves?"

"Our job is to analyze the décor, the color schemes, the theme, and the client buyer's taste to pitch him or her on as many pieces of art as we can."

"Do I carry your sample books?"

"That's all digital these days. You might try to look like you're packing heat."

The phrases of a generation. Would someone twenty years younger say *packing heat*? "A meaningful bulge," he said.

"Actually, you could be helpful. You're a visual guy. That's what you've done for a living, just on pages not on walls."

"I don't speak Mexican."

"Neither do I, but in this case the developers are Chinese. Three days should do it."

They traveled well together. Chandra brought the backgammon case. Patrick got to use his polite Cantonese, which pleased the clients. Chandra did her job well. She was excellent at closing. Except for their separate hotel rooms, they were together constantly. It wasn't hard. The work was fun. Patrick's sole concern in traveling was border crossing with his stash. He needed just enough to hold off withdrawal, a black-tar marble. Chandra hid it in her mascara kit. Fancy restaurant meals and their evenings free. Oaxaca had not totally succumbed to just-another-cityhood. After Oaxaca, they went on to Veracruz, where Meredith had some potential customers she was pitching, and in search of more Mexican art.

When they returned to Twin Peaks, Meredith was not yet back from her trip. She had stopped in New York. Chandra was home only a day before heading out again, this time without Patrick, for Salt Lake City. With neither of them there, the house became foreign. Patrick fit in only as a guest, and now he was the guest of no one. This could never be Patrick's house. It was far too perfect, too pretty, too feminine, like a house dressed up for a date. When the all-female cleaning crew showed up, he hid in his guest room. He had forgotten how vacuous American television was; well, all television probably, but he had barely watched in Asia. Game shows and cop shows and commercials and too many channels, some channels only commercials. The noise of racing American voices hurt his ears. He had to get out of the house. He was tired of taxi cabs. He took one to a car rental place and rented a car. It was cheaper than cabs. He headed out of town, north across the Golden Gate.

On his first visit to Mendocino, Patrick had slept in the woods. This time he found a room in an inn. They had had a cancellation. A Pacific storm was forecast, more seasonably unsettled weather. A honeymoon couple had opted for elsewhere. Patrick got the honeymoon suite with the circular mirror on the ceiling above the king-size bed. Mendocino hadn't changed, the closest California gets to New England colonial. The cliffs and the sea and the seabirds were still the same. The weather was nasty. The inn had a restaurant and a comfy, wood-paneled lounge with an ageing hippie bartender who liked to chat. And there was Ben, the grey-haired local lawyer on the end stool, who sipped endless Irish coffees and had facts or opinions on everything. Male companionship, no rules or obligations attached.

When Patrick returned to his room on his second night there, he noticed he'd gotten a call and a voicemail on his cell phone, which he had left on the dresser. It was from Meredith: "Where are you? Call me." It wasn't that late. He called.

Back when Meredith was Daisy, she talked in the interrogative. Most of her statements were questions. If she was hungry, it was *What's for lunch?* If she wanted to go somewhere, it was *Why don't we go there?* If she wanted advice, it was *If you were me, what would you do?* And, of course, constant queries about names and reasons and causes. She was like a small bird in a nest, her beak always open for more information. When she got older, she had a way of asking personal questions about things that were none of her business. "Just curious," she'd say.

So, it should have come as no surprise to Patrick that on the phone she sounded like a detective.

"Why didn't you answer when I called?" She couldn't conceive of someone being separated from their cell phone.

"I was at dinner without it."

"A little late for dinner, isn't it? You sure you didn't just ignore my call? Will you be home tonight?"

"No. Are you home?"

"Got back this afternoon. What did you have for dinner?"

"Steak."

"Where? Where are you, anyway?"

"I'm at an inn up in Mendocino."

"What? What are you doing there?"

"Staying in the honeymoon suite."

There was a long silence. Silences are longer over the phone, dead-air time echoes. "Are you alone?"

"Yes, I am alone."

"Is Chandra with you?"

"No. She's in Salt Lake City, I think, at least she was. Why do you ask?"

"You two seem to be everywhere together. Hanging out here at the house, then off to Mexico together, then I get back and you're both gone. What am I supposed to think?"

"Well, she's not here, Meredith. Why not give her a call and find out where she is?"

"Maybe I will." Another long pause. "Why would you think I'd be okay with this, Uncle Rick?"

"Okay with what?"

"With you and Chandra."

Chapter 15

"Actually, I didn't know it, but I got to know you, a little bit, before I met you. I mean, I didn't know it was you," Chandra said. They were back at her favorite spot in the house, on the small balcony off the living room. She had her binoculars, for her "beatific surveillance" of the neighborhoods below. They were drinking Chardonnay. Patrick was on a heroin float. It was late in a fine afternoon. "I didn't know that Uncle Rick was also Buck Patrick."

"Buck Patrick?"

"You don't know Buck Patrick? You mean she never…?" Chandra put down her wine and went into the house. She came back with a hardcover book, a volume of Joanna's collected poems called *Fly Ways*. She opened the book to where the back-slipcase flap with Joanna's youthful photo had been folded into the pages. "Let me introduce you to Buck Patrick."

The poem Chandra read was long by Joanna's standards and more narrative than usual, but it was her voice, jumping from image to image, showing rather than telling a story. There was a person—or was it an animal?—named Buck Patrick, who—which? –wandered into and out of the frame of her painting of a place Patrick recognized as the mesa. At one point it was up on her roof, either tearing or repairing it. It blew in through broken windows. It flew away with things she didn't miss till later. It grew horns and shed them. In the end, it had never been there and the mesa was swallowed by fog.

"Read it again," Patrick said. Chandra did.

"Do you understand it?" he asked. "I mean, could you explain it to me?"

"No, but I feel it. It took me a while to see it was you. You represented all those things to her, things she tried to use to define a place but that never came together, just pieces, like memories, not an answer."

"Is it a good poem?" he asked.

"I keep going back to it. It's haunting, the empty expectations."

Every day, FedEx and UPS parcels arrived at the front door. The house was Chandra's office, though she called it home base. Patrick told her the proper term was home plate, and she deferred and henceforward called it that. An Internet slave, when she was home she worked hard, at all times of day, as her clients and potential clients occupied a span of time zones. She had the sleep habits of a lighthouse keeper. Patrick brought in the deliveries and fixed her snacks. Meredith returned to her regular schedule—gone at dawn for her long commute to Palo Alto and seldom home for dinner. It was a big house. Meredith became a stranger. One night, as Patrick passed her room, he heard classical music and stopped outside her door to listen. His long-term memory had started enjoying flashes and blackouts. The piece she was playing occasioned a flash. He didn't know its name, not even its composer, but it was a piano concerto he had heard on many nights forty years before, drifting down from Joanna's up on the mesa, the piano resting, then coming back on attack.

Chandra came home from a day-trip to Las Vegas in a foul mood. She rejected what Patrick fixed her for supper, called him—accurately—a kitchen klutz, and went off to her room like a teenager. As Patrick scraped supper into the garbage disposal, he reminded himself of his dad's advice, don't try to figure them out. He was out on the balcony, having a drink, listening to the murmur of the city hive in the lights below when she came out to join him.

"How do you put up with women, Patrick?"

"The alternatives all involve jail time."

"I considered some of those today. The bitch."

"Do I want to hear this?"

"Why not?"

"It might sour my benign opinion of the fairer sex."

"How many wives have you had?"

"Okay. Go ahead, but no names. Keep it abstract."

"No names necessary. It's a class, no, a set of women. It's almost chemical. We know it when we see each other. This is war."

"Cats can be like that."

"Not only does everything she says and does irritate me, it's intended to, and I give it right back."

"I think I've witnessed that."

"Not good for business when she's your client."

"Drop her."

"I have. I told her to go fuck herself, actually. Normally

I save that for men. But she was just insufferable today. It's come up before, and it will come up again. I deal with more women these days, and too many of them got to where they are by being, well, professional bitches. And there's something about me that brings it out."

"Don't take it so personally. Try feeling sorry for them. What miserable lives they must lead."

"No. They love the way they've become to get where they are. They've left worse behind."

"I guess there isn't a pill for it."

"No, but there is a solution."

"Oh?"

"Have someone else deal with the bitches. You know Robert Louis Stevenson?"

"Never met. Wrote *Kidnapped*."

"Well, when he and his wife Fanny travelled—and they travelled a lot—they had a drill if they ran into trouble. If the trouble causer was a male, Fanny dealt with it. If it was a woman, Louis did."

And thus, Patrick joined the firm as Bitch Tender. It would involve travel and evenings playing backgammon.

Patrick left when the fight broke out. He drove to North Beach and had to park where he'd get a ticket. He walked to Specs. The last thing he had heard as he left the house was Chandra loudly declaiming, as if at a closed door, "I am not your mother."

It was a nice enough second-floor one-bedroom on Stockton near North Point, brand new. It smelled of paint and untrod carpets. They couldn't put a sign on the door because the building wasn't zoned for business, only residential. But it wasn't a walk-in kind of business anyway. Chandra had gotten some sort of deal on the place. Most of the other apartments were still unoccupied. She had had it with working from home and had rented this place as her new home plate. It was part of the peace deal she'd worked out with Meredith. That and Patrick's removal. It was past time.

Patrick didn't live there. He just showed up to help with the mail and deliveries and paperwork. Occasionally, if he missed the last ferry to Sausalito, he would crash there. There was a bed in the bedroom and basic kitchen stuff, but it was really just an office, with desks, computers, filing cabinets, and an answering machine. Strangely enough, given the nature of the business, there was no art on the walls. Patrick was living on a rental houseboat over in Sausalito. The office was only a two-block walk from the ferry dock. Yes, he was back to being a ferry commuter. That was part of how it all came together after he left the Twin Peaks house.

The trip between North Point and Sausalito was shorter than the old Cheung Chau route, but equally pleasant. There wasn't a first-class lounge, but there was a bar, and he could take his drink out onto the fantail, with Alcatraz passing on one side and the Golden Gate on the other. He would buy a bag of chips and feed them to the gulls that hovered above and snatched them out of the air. It was about a mile hike from the ferry dock to his houseboat berth. He was walking again. He lost some weight.

Patrick was now accompanying Chandra on almost all of her road trips, even when there were no female clients to deal with. His duties had expanded. He got to go places he would have never otherwise even considered visiting, like Anchorage and Little Rock, not that any place was very different from the next. The key to their traveling compatibility was that they both prized privacy. Their partnership worked because of boundaries. Also, she was the boss. He deferred to her, held doors for her. They always had separate hotel rooms, and, now that they didn't share a house, there was nothing domestic about their interactions. She always called him Patrick; he always called her Chandra.

They never talked about their pasts, themselves. He had slipped up once and mentioned his son. He was careful not to repeat that sort of mistake. She never went there again, and he never presumed to ask her about what came before they met. It was none of his business. About all Patrick knew of Chandra's past was that she had changed her name. He didn't even know where she was from. There was something vaguely Southern—or was it New England?—about how *r*'s disappeared in certain words. Their pasts were unimportant. What preceded was unnecessary. There was always something better to talk about.

Although the bulk of Chandra's business was in what was called the "hospitality industry," a growing number of her customers were corporations—art for lobbies, offices, waiting rooms. Sometimes this involved brokering for real art, not just off-the-rack stuff, or even commissioning specific pieces. Most often this meant dealing with mid-level corporate trolls who had neither taste nor use for art. It was just decoration to them, not even entertainment, a business expense. But they were afraid of screwing up, so they hired a consultant/supplier to blame if their equally clueless bosses chose to find fault.

Patrick had never been involved in sales before. He had always been paid for his service, his skills, such as they were, at getting things into print. Sales were different. You weren't producing anything; you were just making money by taking something from one person and giving it to someone else. The more artificial value you could add to whatever it was you were transferring, the better for you. Profit without production, the rewards of exaggeration. This suited Chandra fine.

"Profit is god these days," she said. "Nothing else really matters besides the bottom line."

"That's new?"

"Maybe not, but there's less hypocrisy about it now." Chandra shrugged. "People aren't afraid to admit it. Greed is good. It's what keeps the economy running."

"Sin isn't what it used to be."

"I don't think that's a problem either," she said. "Churches pretty much ran that whole sinner thing into the ground. No one believes in hell or purgatory anymore."

They were seated in a lounge at San Francisco International, having a drink while they waited to board their delayed flight for Omaha.

"Sinners in the hands of an angry god," Patrick said.

"Right, Salem witch trials—horror movie stuff, Halloween fare."

"How do they scare kids into behaving these days?"

Chandra shrugged again. "Threaten to take their PlayStation away? No, the shame of greed and pride and the other stone-tablet no-nos like swearing or lying or coveting your neighbors' stuff has been shed like a husk—liberation! —just like all the sexual guilt trips before it."

"Leviticus be damned." Patrick raised his glass in toast.

"Even damning has lost its punch," Chandra said, but she clinked glasses anyway. "And sin has transmogrified, grown wings."

Even the inevitable can be unexpected. Chandra brought the news to the office. "I thought you would have heard." Meredith's mother had died. "Meredith didn't tell you? Two days ago."

Patrick and Meredith had not spoken since Patrick left the Twin Peaks house. Nothing hostile, they had just passed into another phase of incommunicado. He called her from the office. Chandra had her cell phone number. Joanna's body was at a Marin mortuary. There would be a cremation. There would be no funeral. No, there was nothing he could do. "Welcome to the orphan class," he told her.

Back on his houseboat, Patrick chased the dragon thrice. It was time to go away. In a way, he was surprised that the news of Joanna's death had registered so deeply. Hadn't she already passed away in his thoughts when he left her asleep in the nursing home? It was not like she was an ex-lover or even related. It had been thirty years since their last laugh together. But something was now missing. There was a sinkhole where once there had been some certainty. Yes, death was to be feared—not your own, but of those who gave your life meaning. The void that Joanna's passing had revealed was a void that had always been there—mother.

Patrick had never known a mother. His birthing had killed the woman who bore him, and his father never remarried. His sister, just a year older, had gone to an aunt on Long Island, and his father had raised him alone in that flat on Amsterdam Avenue. Growing up, he had hidden the fact that he had no mother, ashamed that that made him different from everyone else. No schoolmates or streetmates were ever invited up to his flat, because there was no mother there. He grew up not knowing a mother's cooking or attention. His dad did as much as he knew how to do, then gave up. All Patrick knew about his mother was that her name was Marie and that she looked tiny in white beside his strapping father in the one, wedding day, photo of her.

There was nothing in the *Chronicle* or the *Examiner* about Joanna's death. Poets don't rate such coverage. The next day, Patrick went into the office. He was helping Chandra arrange the details for their next trip, this time to Hawaii. After work, he caught a ride with her back to Twin Peaks. Meredith was home. Her boss had insisted she take some days off. They had a pizza delivered for dinner. Patrick knew nothing about the so-called stages of grief. Meredith seemed subdued to him, normal if numb. Perhaps one of her pills. She wasn't drinking. She said she was pleased he had come. She took all the pepperoni slices off her piece of pizza and put them on his.

"I guess you are the only family I have left now, Uncle Rick."

"But you're not real family are you, Patrick?" Chandra asked.

"No, I was adopted."

"But long enough ago that the niceties of reality have faded," Meredith said.

"Is anyone planning a memorial service?" Chandra asked.

"Not that I've heard," Meredith said, "and just as well. She never went to anyone else's. Her Bolinas crowd is all gone. I don't think anyone reads her poetry anymore. Nobody cares about poetry."

As Patrick was leaving, Meredith walked him to the door. "Uncle Rick, Thursday, are you busy? I thought I would pick up her ashes. Would you come along?"

"Sure, certainly. Where shall we meet?"

"The place is in San Rafael. I can pick you up in Sausalito on the way."

"Call, and I'll give you directions. There's a café on Bridgeway where we can meet so you won't have to penetrate the houseboat docks warren."

"Actually, I'd like to see your floating nest, but you've never invited me."

"No one has been there. It's not much of a nest. What time?"

"I'll call." She gave him a hug. "Thanks for coming."

The wind was right, steady and strong at their backs. They had walked almost to the center of the bridge, on the ocean side. It was a different climate up here. They were in and out of the racing fog, with splashes of blue sky and flashes of sunlight and sudden sea vistas. It was five degrees colder. There weren't many other sightseers. They had parked on the Marin side. It was all sort of spontaneous, unplanned. They had picked up the box of ashes at the San Rafael mortuary and were driving back to the city when Meredith exited into the overlook parking lot. They hadn't talked much. Meredith seemed preoccupied. She had refused to purchase a proper urn—one in every price range. They sat for a while in silence.

"Mom was such a Marin person," Meredith said. Then she got out of the car and took the box from the back seat.

Patrick joined her, and they hiked out onto the Golden Gate. The wind whipped all that was left of Joanna straight out to sea. An elderly gent on a bicycle saw what they were doing and stopped, doffing his cap in respect.

Chapter 16

It was Patrick's second stay in Waikiki. The first time he had been detoxing and he might as well have been in an air-conditioned hotel room anywhere. He never left it. This time, he was barely in his room except to sleep. It was a brand-new market for Chandra, and she kept him busy. She wasn't staying at his hotel. She was staying with a friend, somewhere outside the city. So, after working hours he was on his own, no backgammon games.

He had expected Waikiki to be something like Miami Beach, but with a dead volcano at one end. He was wrong. First off, it did not feel like part of America, in spite of all the mainland shops and familiar fast-food joints. Part of Asia maybe, as fully half the people there looked Asian. There was the neon flash and bling of Las Vegas. Or was it Macau? The main boulevard ran along the beach, where his high-rise hotel was, pumped with the energy and crowds of Times Square, only with palm trees and an ocean where south of 42nd Street would be.

On his first evening stroll down that raucous boulevard, Patrick had been offered not just tours and take-out menus and complimentary tickets, but also pearls, gold, marijuana, a "date," and a blow job. Even the traffic was midtown dense, though with more stretch limos than taxi cabs. The pedestrian crowds, however, did not have that Manhattan flow, but got clogged up and confused and sometimes stopped altogether around vendors or street mimes or proselytizing evangelicals. And, of course, the plebe minions were ridiculously dressed, as only tourists in their package-tour paradise dared dress. An expositionist clown competition and a pickpocket's version of heaven.

The second night there, after a too-expensive meal, he spent hours wandering the streets of this strange contained peninsula, once a sand spit. Was there ever another place so dedicated to serving strangers? True, the service was generally preemptive and reluctant, but that only insured that no one escaped feeling a stranger, even to themselves. Anonymity was the safety zone for both the served and the servant alike. It was a fake place, a place where no one belonged and no one was their true self. It was the sort of place Patrick had always feared he would end up—a ghetto of the disconnected, a terminal for the hopelessly homeless. The lowest among them haunted the back streets.

It was a big jolt. It woke him, then kept shaking. Out of instinct, he grabbed onto the bed. He waited. Time did one of its stop-and-pay-attention tricks. Two thoughts passed through Patrick's mind—one was of those cheap-motel-room, quarter-operated, "Magic Finger" beds from the 60s; the other was that the moment of death would be like this, frozen to define forever. He was awake enough to remember he was not in San Francisco. The drapes were drawn, but he could tell the sun was out. The digital clock on the nightstand said a little after seven, then it went blank. He was on the twelfth floor. There wasn't much swaying, just shaking and creaking. When it stopped, he got up and opened the drapes, then got dressed, the pants and sport shirt that were on the chair. He was in the dark in the bathroom taking a piss when the second shock hit, as strong as the first. He was knocked sideways, missing the toilet, pissing on the floor. He braced himself against a tile wall. When that jolt rumbled to an end, he went to the room door and opened it, just to see if it would. The corridor was dark. He shut the door.

It was Sunday, a day off. Patrick was drinking a mixture of papaya juice and Stolichnaya from the mini-fridge and chasing his first dragon when Chandra called, checking to see if he was alright. He told her the power was off. She said he should come to where she was and gave him a Kahala Avenue address. The elevators were not working, but there were emergency lights in the stairwell all the way to street level. The only damage at avenue-level seemed to be that traffic lights weren't working, and there was lots of honking. There also seemed to be an awful lot of people out on the street and the beach for so early on a Sunday morning.

It wasn't a very long cab ride, around Diamond Head crater and along the ocean to an avenue of fenced or walled-off and luxuriously planted estates. Nothing seemed disturbed here, the tranquility of wealth. There was a closed gate at his address, and Patrick had the cabbie drop him at the curb. A fresh ocean breeze, bird song, and the distant shriek of a leaf blower. The gate was closed but unlatched, and Patrick let himself in. The driveway to the house was bordered by giant ferns and overarched by palm trees. Chandra met him at the door. She was wearing just a sort of sarong, tied behind her neck.

"How are things in Waikiki?" she asked.

"Lots of tourists thrilled to have a free adventure thrown into their holiday package deal. Selfies all around."

"Damage?"

"None that I could see. Power still out. I guess there's no tsunami. I always wanted to see one of those," Patrick said.

"That's not funny," a voice from behind Chandra said, "not when you live on the beach."

"Patrick has his own brand of humor, Raymond," Chandra said.

It had been a glass sculpture. Now it was a spray of chunks and shards reflecting and prisming sunlight beside an empty pedestal. "I'm thinking of leaving it there, a new installation called *Sic transit*," Raymond said, "only I know the cleaning girls wouldn't allow it." He was taking photographs. "Insurance." It was a long, wide room leading to a wall of windowed doors looking out at a sloping lawn with just the ocean beyond. There were Persian carpets on the floor and more art on the walls. Patrick had the feeling he was there contrary to Raymond's wishes.

"It was a nice enough earthquake, but hardly a disaster," Raymond said. "No need for drastic action. I understand our lady governor has declared a state of emergency. A bit of an overreaction, I'd say, playing up to Pele. She'll be tossing virgins into Kilauea next. You're from New York, Patrick. I can tell by your accent. What do they do with their excess virgins there?"

From his receding hairline, Patrick put Raymond's age close to his own. Gray linen shorts, a subdued aloha shirt, the de rigueur Hawaiian tan. He wore his gayness like a cape.

"Drinks?" Raymond asked. "It is a bit early, but this is an

emergency. Refugees and all."

"Why don't we have something to eat first?" Chandra said.

Brunch was served on the lanai by a slight Filipino, whom no one addressed. Mid-meal, Raymond's cell phone buzzed. He looked at it, said "Excuse me," and left the table, going into the house. Patrick and Chandra talked shop. One of them needed to go to Maui. Patrick volunteered. It had to be better than Waikiki.

"This is a pretty nice billet you have here. Be a shame to leave it," he said.

"There's a Mrs. Chan to deal with there," Chandra said. "When we spoke on the phone, she wanted to talk to my boss, didn't want to deal with a woman."

"I'll fly over tomorrow. Maybe I'll meet a Hawaiian there. I haven't met one yet."

Raymond was coming back to the table. "Be careful what you wish for." He was carrying three tall glasses. The Filipino followed him, carrying a frosted pitcher. "Emergency rations, Margaritas." He gestured for the man to put the pitcher down and clear the table, then he poured their drinks and resumed his seat. "Patrick, I assume from your Christian name and physical type that you are of Irish descent?"

"Safe assumption, pretty much right, a German wife in there somewhere."

"And from New York City. Our father did not have a very elevated opinion of the Irish, did he, sis? An attitude he inherited—unexamined—from his father, a patriarch not averse to letting it be known what or whom he disliked. Granddad's fatal heart attack was occasioned by Kennedy's election."

"He liked Senator McCarthy well enough," Chandra said, watching Patrick over the rim of her glass.

"An essential part of being a man was knowing who your enemy was," Raymond said, "and throughout history your natural enemy has always been the people who do not look or talk or smell like you. For my father, 'black Irish' meant negro."

"Father was not a happy man," Chandra said.

"Thanks to mother."

"Raymond, I don't think Patrick wants to view the family skeletons," Chandra said.

"But of course he does. Dirt on his boss's background. Tell me, Patrick, are you proud of your Irish heritage?"

"I'm not ashamed of it, not that it means that much to me."

"Never visited your homeland?" Raymond refreshed his drink.

"No."

"It's a beautiful place. Charming people. But then, most people are charming when they're where they belong."

"Do you belong here, Raymond?" Chandra asked.

"No, and I'm not charming. But then, neither are the Hawaiians, and they do supposedly belong here."

"Let's not go there, Raymond."

Raymond's phone went off again, and again he went off into the house with it. Chandra got up and walked down the steps to the lawn, gesturing with her head for Patrick to follow. They strolled oceanward.

"I'm afraid my brother is feeling threatened," Chandra said.

"By what? By my being Irish?"

"By reality. When dad died, Raymond was saddled with too much. He wasn't ready for it. That bit about enemies is where he's retreated to—looking for enemies everywhere. His latest foes are Hawaiians."

"But he would seem to have everything."

"He's always had everything. He's afraid the great *they* want to take it away."

"No one can take his privilege away."

"What privilege is that?"

"Of being a pampered white male in America." There were steps leading down to the beach. They stopped there and sat on the steps.

"Raymond hardly had control over that," Chandra said. "Personally, I'm rather glad I was born white. Aren't you? And my *privileges* have been hard won over many generations."

"What's he got against Hawaiians?"

"A group on the Big Island is blocking one of his projects by claiming cultural significance for an archaeological site there. Raymond thinks it's all bullshit."

"And you?"

"Not my fight. Although, nobody thought the site was worth anything until he bought it and started development. Then suddenly it was like Chartres Cathedral."

Raymond never reappeared. There were no more earthquakes. The power had come back on. Chandra offered to call Patrick a cab, but it was a beautiful afternoon and it couldn't be more than a few miles back. He was in no hurry to return to Waikiki. He'd walk. It was more than a few miles. Maybe four? It took him more than an hour, but it was a pleasant hike, mainly along the ocean, with a sea breeze all the way until he hit the high-rise hotels. He stopped for a drink at the first place he could. The place dripped with island décor—tiki heads and surf boards, paintings of hula dancers. The bartender was big and brown, in an aloha shirt, his jet-black hair pulled back in a shaggy ponytail.

"Excuse me for asking," Patrick said, "but are you Hawaiian?"

"You excused, man. No, I'm no Hawaiian, bro. More better, I'm Samoan."

Mrs. Chan in Maui was no problem. Patrick's Cantonese helped. Chandra considered the entire trip a success, and they flew back together first class to San Francisco. Free champagne. Patrick disliked champagne and gave his to Chandra, who belonged in first class, was at home there. She kicked off her shoes and asked for another pillow. She nested in the window seat. She was aghast at how bad the art was in Hawaii hotels. "Of course, the distractions there are not indoors like in Las Vegas, but still. Did you notice the total absence of seascapes?" Patrick had never seen her so relaxed. "God, it's good to get out of there." She ordered another flute of bubbly.

The only places most Americans can still enjoy the feudal pleasure of having servants are in up-scale restaurants and first-class travel, a vestigial pleasure for a culture conceived by slave holders, a rare treat for most. Their flight attendant became Chandra's vassal. It was natural. They both knew their roles. When the attendant did something for Patrick it was a favor, but she seemed to read Chandra's mind.

"In the future, Patrick, I think I'll let you deal with Hawaii. The place makes me uncomfortable, the people, I guess. It's so…it's too…I don't know what to call it…Asian, I guess, and I don't even know what that means. I've never been there—Asia, that is. You lived there a long time. What is it I'm feeling? Am I just over-reading the inscrutable East thing?"

"I don't know. They're just people. Compared to Americans, Asian business people tend to be more patient. They play the long game. They keep their egos out of it, always cordial, but that doesn't mean they can't be trusted. In my years there, no one ever tried to screw me over, not professionally anyway."

"Most of the people I dealt with were Japanese. Dad hated the Japanese." Chandra took a sip of champagne and looked out her window at the nothing that is all there ever is to see out of airplane windows at cruising altitude. "Even though he made most of his money off the war."

Chandra's attendant came and placed a tray of fruit and cheese on her service tray. Patrick had to stop her to ask for a fresh drink.

"It's not other cultures," Chandra said. "I don't feel that way when I'm dealing with Europeans, even Mexicans. I wonder what Russians are like?"

After dinner, Chandra took a nap, curled up in her recliner throne. Her attendant brought a blanket for her. Patrick watched her sleep. He liked watching women sleep, peaceful, defenseless, harmless. Many women were more beautiful asleep, unguarded, untouchable innocence. Chandra was one of them.

Six hours is a long time to be strapped in a seat, no matter how comfortable it is. Patrick fondly remembered the old days—yes, he was an old guy now; he got to do that—

the old days with the 747 upstairs lounge. On his first trip to Asia in '76, a ten-hour haul from Honolulu to Manila, he had spent most of the flight, save for takeoff and landing, on a bar stool in the upstairs lounge, playing bar dice, chatting with stewardesses, and drinking rusty nails with a Manila businessman in a Rolex and many jeweled rings, who offered him a job selling real estate. Now, if you got up to stretch your legs, they thought you were a terrorist. Now, they probably didn't have a bottle of Drambuie on the plane.

Patrick took some days off when they got back. He and Chandra had been together for too many days. The job was beginning to feel like work. He stayed on his houseboat and in Sausalito. There really wasn't much to his houseboat. It was more boat than house. He only occasionally bumped his head. It wasn't a party boat. Jerry, the guy who had built it and was letting Patrick stay there for a monthly donation—he wasn't allowed to rent—had planned it as a "love nest getaway" for himself and a woman who left him before it was finished. There was a blank space on the stern where her name was to have gone. Patrick burned patchouli incense to cover the smell of mold. There was a lovely sundeck, often a fogdeck. There was plenty to do if he wished to. All involved sandpaper, stains, brushes, and rags. The story was Patrick was living aboard to finish the boat. But no one from the houseboat association ever stopped by to check. Some sunsets, if it was clear, Jerry would stop by with a couple of quarts of green death and a doobie to sit on the deck and shoot the breeze.

Then one day, a Sunday, it turned out, Meredith called.

How about lunch? They met at a place in Sausalito, and after lunch Meredith drove Patrick back to his dock. She wanted to visit his keep.

"You never have owned much of anything, have you, Uncle Rick?" Daisy still asked hard-to-answer questions.

"Never got in the habit," he said.

The view from the deck was of other houseboats, some fancy, some funky.

"What are your neighbors like?"

"Quiet mostly, polite, standoffish, all good qualities in neighbors. It's like New York in a way. When you live so close together, you learn to prize privacy. I really don't know anyone here."

"Mom never did like neighbors who acted like family. When you came back to the mainland, why didn't you go back home, to Manhattan?"

"Home is a place you grow out of," he said.

"Like a hermit crab exchanging shells?" Another one of those questions.

"I like it here," he said.

A small boat passed, broadcasting a low wake that swayed them like a whisper.

"Do you think I would like it in New York?"

"I think you'd do fine there. Why?"

"I've been offered a job there. HarperCollins."

"Good job? Why not take it? Bigger shell."

"It would mean leaving here, leaving Chandra."

Leaving. Ah, there's the rub. For some, departures were not a gate but a moat, while for others, departures were a bridge across that moat. The gates at an airport—Arrivals, Departures. Binary, yin-yang, one cannot exist without the other. Most Americans die in their birth county, which they never left.

"You'll like New York. You're ready for it. You've even got an invitation. Most people don't."

"I haven't told Chandra."

Chapter 17

Patrick couldn't believe it. It was pristine inside its little plastic envelope. Patrick checked the back. Yes, it was the '69 card, because the previous year's stats on the back were for the disastrous '68 season when he batted only .217 after Bob Gibson beaned him in spring training. Tommie Agee, the center fielder for the Miracle Mets of '69, when he led the team in homers and RBIs and, in Patrick's opinion, saved the Series with his defense in game three. Boy, was that a memorable Series. Only three bucks. He had to own it.

Chandra liked flea markets. Who knew? A Sunday off in Austin. She had wandered away, looking for bargains. Patrick babysat his boredom by flipping through boxes of old baseball cards, like memory flashcards. Those repeated stock poses—pitcher, catcher, slugger, fielder. How the caps and the uniforms changed. He bought a Luke Easter, too.

What kind of capitalism was this? Did it have a name? A market of the totally unnecessary. Worthless things on sale for less, a glut of discards changing hands. On this acre of vendors there was not one item for sale that anyone actually needed. Nothing to eat, nothing to drink, no implement, ointment, objet d'uh, or piece of attire that you had not been happily living without. He tucked his two new possessions into his shirt pocket.

When Patrick came back to the States, he had to ask about

all the storage facilities that had sprung up in the suburbs. Storage of what? Wait. People were paying to rent space to stash all the stuff that they couldn't fit into their oversized houses and garages? That was crazy. Life, liberty, and the pursuit of stuff? Stuff like this? Excess stuff. It was like a material extension of the departure problem, the inability to say goodbye. How many internal-combustion devices can one man acquire? How many clothes can one woman wear? Chandra returned with a black lace mantilla. "Did someone die?" Patrick asked.

She also had a small wooden box covered with sea shells, "for Meredith." Of course, sea shells from Austin. Patrick was high. It was Sunday, the traditional day for worshipping whatever you got. Chandra knew he was high. He made no secret of it. It was how she had managed to drag him to the flea market. She seemed to enjoy his company when he was flying. She played with it. It was like he was her pet for a while, if he let her. Stoned, Patrick didn't mind. It was a fun enough game, playing her distracted sidekick, her second banana. He could make her laugh. Chandra had a nice laugh, a laugh that made strangers smile.

People sometimes assumed they were a couple, like married or something. Chandra played with that as well. But that was less fun, more like a '50s sit-com version of an American, husband's-a-dolt marriage. She played that one for female audiences. Patrick would walk away. But there was no audience today.

"That's a nice box," Patrick said. "She'll like that. I remember her as a girl picking up shells on the beach." And throwing them back into the ocean, he thought but didn't say. He could play his own games.

"How old was Meredith when you first got to know her?" Chandra asked.

"AKA Daisy was ten, I believe, in adult years."

"What was she like?"

They had left the flea market and were on a busy boulevard, looking for a place for refreshments.

"Short, a little wise-ass, a bit of a tomboy, I guess. Isn't that strange? In English, most things masculine normally carry a John or Jack assignation. You know—jack of all trades, jackhammer, jack o' nine tails, jackass, John Doe, jack-off. Except for tomboy and tomcat."

"And tomfoolery," Chandra said. "She never talks much about her childhood."

"She may be still trying to figure it out. It looked pretty confusing to me. Or—she's a smart cookie—maybe she just decided to ditch it."

It wasn't ideal, but it would do. One-page plastic menus, but it had a full bar. They sat at a patio table and ordered.

"Patrick, what do you think of same-sex marriages?"

"I understand penguins in zoos do it, but they're not Christians, or Americans."

"It's not yet legal, but there is a case headed for the Supreme Court."

"They dress like penguins." His Stoli and tonic arrived.

"Civil ceremonies have become common in San Francisco. Everything but a state-issued license."

"I don't know why the state gets involved at all. What's it to them except a license fee? But then, I'm no longer clear why people want to get hitched in the first place, now that dowries are history."

"It's an additional commitment, Patrick."

"Yeah, exactly. Like hara-kiri." Patrick looked across the table at his companion who suddenly seemed far away. She was studying her drink. He supposed, if you were into possessions, that another human being would be an ultimate prize, better even than a pet. They had struck slavery from the books, but they left matrimony. You hadn't needed a license to own a slave, but you did to claim a mate—a state-sanctioned privilege. Chattel, such a fine old word. *Goin to the chapel and I'm gonna be chattel.* He started humming the old pop song.

Chandra looked up. "What does gender have to do with commitment?"

"Precisely," he said. "And whose business is it besides yours anyway? Meredith?"

"It's time, I think. We've been together seven years now."

"Why change what's working?"

"It's called development, Patrick, progress, the future."

"Oh, I forgot. I always forget the future stuff, the stuff that hasn't happened yet."

"Do you have a problem with my marrying Meredith?"

"No, no, if that's what both of you want. That's your business. I'll even give her away. Now, isn't that an interesting term?"

Their food came in those recycled red plastic baskets which, like everything reusable, made you wonder about its previous users, inventing a past for it, not unlike inventing futures—how would you feel about a stranger wearing your favorite coat, after you no longer needed it? The flea in flea market came with its origin, a place to unload no-longer owned clothes, medievally unlaundered. That coat with the dead man's fleas.

"Have you set a date?" he asked. Isn't that what one was supposed to ask?

"There was one couple on the mesa I liked. They just let me hang out at their place, never any questions, never any bother. They had a library, a room just for books—and a globe. There was a globe." Meredith had her bare feet up on the railing of the sundeck. Only her feet were in the sun. "They were never home during the day. They had real jobs. He was a doctor, and she—her name was Margot—worked in the city. She wrote a column for the *Chronicle*. They were the straightest couple in town. Their house was always locked, but I'd get in through the dog door. They didn't mind. Sometimes they'd leave notes for me, like 'leftovers in the fridge' or 'turn on the crock pot at two.' They were cool. They never reported me to mom. Mom didn't even know I knew them. They didn't have any kids of their own, or maybe they were grown. John—that was the husband's name—would leave books out for me to read, boys' book mainly, like the Hardy Boys or the Hornblower books, Tom Sawyer."

"His favorite books from that age," Patrick said. It was another Sunday, the next one actually. Meredith had called before stopping by, but only after she arrived in Sausalito, to make sure, she said, she wouldn't encounter any of his crazy lady friends. She had been going through some of her mother's things and wanted to share something.

"John liked Shakespeare and Blake. He thought all the local poets were whacko. Margot bought me my first Kotex."

It was a bird that got them to Bolinas. Meredith had brought a bottle of Chardonnay, and they took their glasses out onto the half-shadow sundeck. A large white bird was drifting by in the inter-dock channel.

"Oh, a snow goose," Meredith said. "Those are rare."

"My moat-guard goose," Patrick said. He'd never seen it before.

"Like the one on Merlin's Lane up on the mesa? Mom wanted to kill that bird after it attacked me."

"She warned me off that lane," he said.

"She wrote a poem about it, 'Take a Gander.' It's in the collected."

"I don't have her book," Patrick said.

"She'd want you to. There's at least one poem you appear in."

"Yes, Chandra read it to me."

At the mention of Chandra's name, Meredith switched back to Bolinas memories— "It's all gone now. Hippies, an endangered if not already extinct species"—leading to the story of Margot and John, the only "normal" couple she knew growing up. Meredith put air quotes around normal. "Their normal was its own brand of status-quo weird."

What Meredith had brought to show him was a photograph, a 5 x 7 black-and-white glossy of him and Joanna. They were in profile, waist-up, standing side-by-side, each holding a glass, against what looked like fake sky. They both were young. Patrick looked handsomer than he ever really was. Joanna was glowing in the flash and laughing, her head resting on his shoulder. It was from that poetry reading in Oakland thirty-some years before, where the canvases cascaded.

"She saved this one," Meredith said. "She didn't save many. She had a thing against photographs. 'Frozen time,' she called them. There are none of me growing up."

Patrick shared Joanna's unease with old personal photographs. They weren't inert like baseball cards. They were keys to doors best left locked. For some, the past was not nostalgic. His dad had never even owned a camera. There were no family photo albums. Yearbook pictures, ID cards, passport photos, an SFPD mug shot—a slim, lost history of headshots. In most of them he had been wearing a tie. There were no snaps of him smiling, not even this one—just a blank expression. He handed the photo back to Meredith.

"No, keep it. That's yours," she said. "I had a copy made. I thought you might want it."

"Thanks." He didn't know what he would do with it. "What's up with the HarperCollins gig?"

"That's on hold while I finish some projects at the Press. I'm replacing someone there who hasn't left yet."

"Ready for the Big Apple?"

"I think so. San Francisco has gotten, I don't know, too much like L.A. It's sold out. Bling is everything."

"You think New York will be any less so?"

"More diverse anyway, and new. Besides, New York is just living up to its reputation. San Francisco has lost its."

"Winters?" Patrick said.

"Warmer clothes," Meredith said.

"Subways?"

"No more one-hour commutes."

"No big house on Twin Peaks?"

"That has always been Chandra's house, not mine." Meredith took Patrick's glass and hers into the galley to refill.

When she returned with them, Patrick asked, "Chandra?"

"Chandra has her own life. She'll find another

housemate."

"Does she know you are leaving?"

"I think she suspects it. I haven't told her yet."

"Why not?"

"No firm departure date."

The snow goose was still out there, cruising now in the opposite direction like a good guard goose.

Lorenzo was gone. This posed a problem. Patrick didn't know where else to go for his black tar. He stretched out what he had left, coming off slowly. Chandra scored him some cocaine and methadone, which helped. When he asked her where, she just smiled and said, "compliments of the hospitality community." He muddled through. Withdrawal was like the flu. He stayed on the boat. He had to miss their next trip, a long one. He was getting too old for this shit. When he got clean, he'd stay off; just ethanol and cannabis and maybe some cocaine now and then. Become one of them. He wondered if psilocybin was still available, Fungod tours.

When Patrick felt well enough to get off the boat, he stayed on the water. He took to riding the ferries, not just the Sausalito-San Francisco route, but the boats to Tiburon and Alameda as well. He liked being out on the bay, with the gulls and the views and the wind you could lean on. He took his meals and his drinks from the snack bar. The gulls got to know him as Mr. Chips. To the tourists and commuters, he was just an old guy in a seaman's cap leaning on the fantail railing, watching the parallel foam troughs of their dual-hull wake spread and meld and vanish behind them.

He was left alone.

Being alone was his default. His fault? His failure? He had lived alone most of his life. He claimed to prefer it. The two times he tried otherwise the women had left him. All along he had felt incomplete, as if he needed a woman to complete him, the proverbial better half. His whole life he had felt the need to hide his incompleteness. But he had learned to be alone without being lonely. Or was it lonesome? He wasn't sure of the difference. He had definitely never felt homesick or lovesick. What he was missing was undefined, nonspecific, an unnamed absence.

In the midst of this withdrawal, the usual trench of depression had seemed especially deep. It had scared him. The cocaine had helped him crawl out, but he had escaped with the message that there was more to jettison than opiates—his delusions. The first delusion was hope. There was no hope; there was just the future. The second delusion was his version of himself as someone from whom something had been withheld. No, his life was a whole. It was what it was. Nothing was missing. He was who he was, no addition could change that. It was way too late for change anyway. What a dupe he had been to think that a mate could have changed anything, that a woman was the answer to anything. What was the question?

Patrick laughed to himself. In a final act of pointless, delusional, chivalrous grandiosity he would free women by not needing them. Emancipation all around. The gulls—in a state of constant, subtle, aerodynamic adjustments that allowed them to hover in the buffeting crosswinds and updrafts as if attached by invisible filaments to his outstretched arm—were now plucking sour-cream potato chips from his fingertips.

In San Francisco Patrick went ashore and hiked through the unfortunate Financial District toward North Beach. It was quitting time, and the streets were full of gentlemen in gray suits with briefcases and gentlewomen in gray suits with briefcases, rushing to escape their jobs. He went to Specs, which was just opening. A young redheaded bartender brought him his green death. Patrick sat at his favorite old spot at the alley-window end of the bar. He wasn't alone, just by himself.

Chapter 18

They were going to miss the plane. Patrick was waiting at the office with his luggage and the files Chandra said she wanted to take, but there was no Chandra. The last he spoke with her, she said she would be there by four, which was already cutting it close. It was now twenty after. Of course, there would be later flights—they were going to Miami—and the cost of the missed reservations would not be coming out of Patrick's pocket, but still.... This was far from the first time Chandra had left him waiting, staring at a clock.

Patrick supposed there were men who habitually kept people waiting, but in his experience they had all been female. His ex had been a master at it. At first, he had written it off as just scatter-mindedness, one of those culturally excusable distaff traits; but he was deluding himself. Of course it was intentional, both tactical and strategic. "Let him wait" might serve some immediate purpose of lassitude, but it also helped train him to accept his proper place as serf. After training a dog to sit, you teach it to stay. Objecting was seen as biting the hand that caressed you.

There was no point in calling her cell phone. The presumption would just piss her off. If she had something to tell him, she would call. Besides, she was probably, or should be, in traffic. Patrick had taken up smoking again. Part of going straight was going straight to replacement addictions.

Chandra, like everyone else in polite society, abhorred even the idea of the smell of cigarette smoke. He had to go outside to light up. There was a small central courtyard planted with things that refused to grow, that did their best just to survive without sunlight. That was depressing. He went out to the sidewalk. The fog was flowing up Stockton Street, but the traffic was moving alright. No Chandra. He checked his cell phone—4:35. There was no way they would make their flight now, not with the security lines this time of day. There was that sea-chill smell in the air.

Patrick was tense, the tension that comes from controlling anger. Fuck the flight, fuck Miami. He despised Miami, America's melanoma. But being stood up pissed him off. Too unimportant to be informed. Well, they wouldn't be going anywhere tonight. At least he wouldn't be. Fuck this. He could hear the Alcatraz foghorn. Let it go, he told himself, as he flicked his butt into the gutter. There was a reason why every so often the peasants slaughtered the nobles. Of course, they were still peasants afterwards. He turned off his cell phone. It was just a half-mile hike to Specs, moving with the fog.

Her English was probably perfect, but it was hard to understand. She had learned it in school, rather than from American TV. She was young and Japanese and very politely asked permission to sit on the barstool next to Patrick's. Then she asked if she could ask him a few questions about North Beach. When he agreed—why not? —she put her cell phone on the bar between them. Patrick assumed she was recording. She had a list written down and she consulted it.

The list was in Japanese. She asked in English.

Maiko knew more about North Beach than Patrick did. He was of little help. She was doing research for her dissertation about the San Francisco poet scene from some university back in Japan. She wished to speak to elders like his honorable self who might have memories about those days. She knew Joanna's work.

Patrick talked to Maiko about Joanna and Bolinas. It helped him calm down. Off the dragon, he had lost the springs between him and reality, and things like getting pissed off lingered on his nerves. He had ordered a double Jameson's with his green death. He had left his luggage at the office and would have to go back there to get it and then lug it home on the last ferry if he didn't miss it, and he didn't want to go back to the office, and screw Chandra anyway.

Maiko didn't know about Bolinas. The name was in her notes, but just as an address, not a mindset. She mispronounced it. The story he told her about Bolinas and Marin made it sound like a paupers' Camelot. He ordered her a draft with his second round, which she only sipped out of courtesy. She took his photograph, discretely, without the flash, and wrote down his name. She asked if he had published poems, and he laughed.

A young Japanese man came to the door and got Maiko's attention. He seemed perturbed. He pointed at his large wristwatch and jerked his head toward the street. She took her time responding, taking a sip of her lager, putting her pad and pen and phone in her purse. When she got up to leave, she shook Patrick's hand and thanked him. He knew enough Japanese to wish her a good evening, which made her smile. Patrick stayed for a few more rounds and missed the last ferry. He crashed at the office.

"Wake up! Why is your phone turned off?" Chandra was shaking his shoulder. "What are you doing here?"

Daylight outside the window. "Why, waiting for you," Patrick said. "You never showed up."

"How could I reach you with your phone turned off? I left messages."

"After the fact," he said.

"There was an...emergency. I've postponed the trip." Chandra noticed that Patrick, now sitting up in bed, was undressed. She turned and left the room, closing the door behind her.

When Patrick, dressed now, joined Chandra in the front room, she was looking at her cell phone. He had his luggage with him. He was headed home.

"Have you heard from Meredith?" she asked.

"Phone turned off, remember?"

"I thought she might be with you when you didn't answer." Chandra was still studying her phone.

"Why would Meredith be with me?"

"She said you understood her," Chandra said, and she looked up at him, "that you wanted her to move forward, weren't trying to hold her back." Chandra wasn't wearing any makeup. Her hair was just pulled back and haphazardly cinched. Her eyes said she had not slept. The scrim that hid her age had fallen away. "You urged her to take the New York job, didn't you?"

"Meredith is free to do as she pleases."

"Things were fine between us before you showed up."

"Really, Chandra."

"Uncle Rick, the free spirit, world traveler, New Yorker, home breaker."

Patrick was standing in the middle of the room, holding his luggage. "I gather Meredith is missing."

"We fought. She left. I have to talk to her. She was so upset. She's making a big mistake." Chandra's phone made a sound, and she glanced at it, then scowled at it and flipped it shut. There were tears in her eyes. "And I thought you were my friend, Patrick."

Patrick headed for the street door. This was where he exited. Wasn't that the basic universal truth, that nothing was permanent? That the only thing that did not change was the certainty of changing? That and the fact that there was always an exit. Whether it was progress or decomposition was a judgement call.

As he left, Chandra said, "If you hear from her, you'll let me know, won't you, Patrick? Please, Patrick, please talk some sense into her, stop her."

The sun was just coming up at the end of North Point Street. Patrick caught the first ferry back to Sausalito. It was almost empty. All the commuters were headed in the opposite direction, and it was too early for tourists. It was chilly on the bay. He got a cup of coffee. There was no smoking allowed onboard, but no one stopped him. Social rules don't apply where there is no society. A loner needed no rules at all. He didn't feature carrying his bag all the way back to the boat, so he caught a cab dropping someone off at the ferry.

"The hatch latch wasn't locked," Meredith said. She was in his bunk, beneath all the blankets.

"It doesn't, but that's a secret," Patrick said.

"I won't tell anyone," she said.

Her presence there was not a complete surprise. He had seen what he thought was her car haphazardly parked at the end of the dock.

"You got any heat in this barge?" she asked, just her head above the covers.

Patrick went back to the galley and turned on the electric space heater. He filled the kettle and turned it on. "You been here all night?" he called back to the bedroom.

"Pretty much. You should wash your sheets. They've got that guy aroma."

Loners don't have any laundry rules, he thought. He got down two bowls and two packets of instant oatmeal. "Maple-brown sugar or apple-cinnamon?" he called.

Meredith came into the galley fully clothed and wrapped in his blanket. "You're still eating the same thing for breakfast. I remember you feeding me that when I stayed with you in that Berkeley garage. I'd never had it before. You called it gruel. I remember thinking, I don't know what Oliver Twist was complaining about."

"Only instant coffee," Patrick said.

"Make it strong then."

The sun was warming the sundeck, and they broke their fast at the table there.

"I missed the last ferry and slept at the office," he said.

"Considerate of you, seeing as I was in your bed. I tried calling, but your phone must have been off, because it went right to voicemail."

"Chandra came by at dawn."

Meredith froze. "What? Why?"

"Haven't the slightest. She was upset."

"She's been calling me. I've blocked her number."

"I'm supposed to talk sense to you," Patrick said.

"Well?"

"Wrong guy. You got a plan?"

Meredith finally cracked. Her voice broke. "No, no plan. I had a plan. I was all packed...." She started sobbing. She sobbed for a while. "I didn't know she would take it so hard. We hadn't been getting along. I thought she'd be angry. I was ready for that." More sobbing. "She pleaded with me to stay. She made promises. We had once agreed there would be no promises, only the present."

Meredith got up and went into the cabin. It took her a while, but when she came back out, she was more composed. "Maybe I did mean to hurt her. If so, I was wrong. She doesn't deserve to be hurt. But then she threatened me."

"With what?" Patrick asked. A threat to him meant violence, a knife or something.

"With revealing things only she knows about me, with trying to sabotage my career. Then we argued, the same old things all over again, and she started screaming and throwing things at me. And I left."

"You said you were packed. Were you ready to go? You have flight reservations?"

"Yes, for this afternoon. But now I don't think I can leave. It doesn't seem right to hurt her so." She started crying again, crying this time, not sobbing. "She had rings, wedding rings."

"No, Meredith, I think you can leave. I think you must leave. You are whole without her. It's time to move on. You'll never forgive yourself, or her, if you don't leave. I'll help you catch that flight." I know all about leaving, Patrick thought. I'm a pro.

It went smoothly, considering how keyed up Meredith was. Patrick had to drive, and at the bridge she wanted to turn back. But when they got to Twin Peaks, Chandra wasn't home. Meredith got her bags. Patrick took them down to the car, but Meredith did not follow. Back in the house, he found her sweeping up pieces of broken ceramics and glass in the hallway. She was weeping.

Patrick took the broom from her hands and said, "No. We go."

She went back to her room and returned with a framed poster. It was Sky Fucker. She handed it to him. "Hang onto this for me, will you?"

On the way to the airport, Meredith was numb. Patrick said he would sell her car for her. She agreed by nodding her head. He dropped her at her departure gate, then went and parked. He wanted to make sure she got on her flight. He caught up with her in the security line. She was looking at her phone.

"My battery is dead," she said.

"You can't use it on the plane anyway."

"The recharger is in my luggage."

"Then you can recharge in New York," he said. "Is someone meeting you?"

"But I wanted to call Chandra, tell her I was going."

"No, you don't. Chandra knows you're gone. Give her time for that to sink in."

"No, I have to tell her personally, hear her voice."

"Plenty of time for that later." The line crept forward.

"Give me your phone."

"No. You're not calling her. You have a plane to catch."

The man in uniform asked to see her boarding pass and passport.

"Call me when you get there and are recharged," Patrick called after her. The last he saw her, she was taking off her shoes.

It wasn't until Patrick got back to the houseboat that he turned his phone back on. He erased all his voicemail and text messages without listening to or reading them. All prelude, all history. He texted Chandra: "Meredith caught her NY flight. Let her go."

He never heard back from Chandra, never saw her again. In fact, he seldom got over to the city or even out of Sausalito. He was busy fixing up the houseboat, finishing it, improving it. Jerry had hinted at maybe selling. Patrick was waiting for the price to come down. Jerry had a new, expensive girlfriend. Why not own a home that could sink or float away? Patrick found a place to hang Sky Fucker.

When he went to town, he would look at San Francisco across the bay, which looked more and more like Oz and less and less like the city he once knew.

John Enright was born in Buffalo, New York in 1945. After serving stints in semipro baseball and the Lackawanna steel mills, he earned his degree from City College of New York while working full-time at *Fortune*, *Time*, and *Newsweek* magazines. He later completed a master's degeee in folklore at the University of California, Berkeley before devoting the 1970s to the publishing industry in New York, San Francisco, and Hong Kong. In 1981, he left the United States to teach at American Samoa Community College. He spent the next twenty-six years living on the islands of the South Pacific, working for environmental, cultural, and historical resource preservation. Over the past five decades, his essays, articles, short stories, and poems have appeared in more than ninety books, anthologies, journals, periodicals, and online magazines. His collection of poems from Samoa, *14 degrees South*, won the University of the South Pacific Press's inaugural International Literature Competition. He lives in Owensboro, Kentucky.